In The M

Once a caterpillar becomes a butterfly, it will never crawl again

Poems

Theresa Bailey McClendon

2004

In The Midst Of....

CONTENTS

Acknowledgements	xiii
Foreword - Perry McClendon Jr.	xv
Foreword - C. Taylor McClendon	xvi
Foreword - Yvette Butcher	xvii
Foreword - God	xviii
From the Author	ix
Dedication	xxi

Section One 　　　"*Nourishment Inside the Cocoon*"　　1

II Corinthians 5:17	3
If you cannot get along......	5
The Original Tree	6
Be Gentle	11
Valley of Decision	13
God Can Handle It	14
Waiting Is Not Easy	17
I Was Hurt	19
The Metamorphosis of the Queen of Bitter	23
Nobody Else Can	25
I Am So Scared	27
The Washing of the Water With the Word	28
He Knows	32
Lend Me Your Hope Lord	34
Doctor Daddy	35
Me, Myself, and I	38
Keep Your Eyes On the Cross	41
You Can Make It	43

Section Two　　　"*The Protection of the Cocoon*"　　46

The Glory Belongs to God	47
True Confessions	50
G.od's R.iches A.t C.hrist's E.xpense	53

The Leper's Song	55
Who Told You - You Were Naked	57
Living Well	60
Questions - Answers	61

Section Three　　　　*"Freedom from the Cocoon"*　　**64**

Why the Caged Bird Could Not Sing	65
My Favorite Songs	66
My First Choice	67
There's Nothing More Exciting Than a Strong Woman	70
Clay Feet In High Heels	74
It Is Well	77
On My Knees	78
Sisters From Another Mother	82
God's Word	84
The Touch	85
Reproduction	89
He Couldn't Carry His	90
Dancing	93
His Just Reward	96
My Friend, My Sister	99
....	100
I Am A Man	103
He'll Fit You For The Task	106
Tribute to My Auntie	108
From the Heart of A Mother	111
A Love Story	113
Psalms 119:71	117
From My Counselor	118
Two Is Better Than One	119
Counseling	121
Resources	123
The Last Word	125

"And out of the ground the LORD God made to grow, every tree that is pleasant to the sight, and good for food; the tree of life also **in the midst of** the garden, and the tree of knowledge of good and evil." Genesis 2:9

"In The Midst Of . . . "

Encouraging mankind everywhere that life is not over when tragedy comes.

"Once a caterpillar becomes a butterfly, it will never crawl again."

Theresa Bailey McClendon

My Personal Testimony in Pursuit of Excellence

"In The Midst Of"

Nurturing, Mentoring, and Encouraging One Another by Sharing.

ACKNOWLEDGEMENTS

I have so many people to thank for this project. I am extremely grateful for all of them. I thank my Lord, who if I had been the only one, He still would have suffered the excruciating death of the cross, just for me. I thank my sons who have seen me display every emotion known to man and they still think highly of me. Go figure. They have heard every word of this book at least three times and they still love it! I highly respect them and esteem them as the precious people they are, may God fill their lives richly as He chooses. I thank my wonderful friend who became my sister, Yvette. You serve as my agent as well but it is your friendship that I treasure. You worked many a night with me on this project. I hear you snoring even as we work and I write! I love you dearly!

To all of you who read, proofed, and listened as I tried to collect my thoughts. Thank you for your biased commentaries. My cousins, Jackie Pounds and Viola McCalla, The Book Group at Barnes and Noble at The Forum, Norcross, GA., my dear sister who is now with the Lord, Andrea Skinner who would call me up ask me to read to her! To Marilyn Mock and Micheala McCarthy, who took the time to read and make written comments, to Coni Brown, my longtime friend and confidant of forty plus years, to Phil and Edwina Thierry, who have always made me feel special for over 25 years! To Diane Poole Thomas and the entire Poole family, your friendship for over 25 years! Ocala, Fla. would not be the same without you! To Pat Adams, thanks for your undying support, you're the best!

To Rob and Peggy Attaway, your photography and technical skills are like you, priceless!

To Allister Akong, the World waits for your fine art work! Thank you.

To countless others, you know who you are! Please know that I love you and I am so grateful for you. You should know how good it is to be loved by you!

To Pastor Erven Kimble of the Central Baptist Church, Lilburn, GA. Your disciplined studying techniques are without comparison. I am grateful.

Last but certainly not least, to the Pastor Lee Smith and The First Baptist Church, Norcross, Georgia where Jesus is Lord to the glory of God. You took my sons and me in and made us feel welcomed. You loved us back to health. Thank you for believing in me and affirming the gift that God has given me. To my Sunday School Class, The Flock!!! I couldn't have done without you! I'll finally bring the treats! You… are in my prayers!

Foreword

When my mother asked me to write the foreword for her book, *"In The Midst Of…"*, I was both flattered and shocked! I was curious as to why she would want me Perry B. McClendon, Jr. her first born, her pride and joy, her baby boy. Then I thought…well, yeah! No wonder she asked *me* to write this foreword for her book.

My mother is my inspiration for my life, without her, I would be lost. I am so happy for her. She has been writing for as long as I can remember. She always ask for my opinion on things making me feel important in everything she attempts. I couldn't ask for a better mother than mine. She is more than a mother to me, she has also been a friend too. I can tell my mom anything and I can ask her for anything…believe me, I do!

This book my mother wrote really paints a picture of the life she leads and models for my brother and me. When you read this book, you will understand and feel the pain and joy my mother has been through. The beauty of it is, you will be pointed to the same source of strength she draws from. I trust when you read this book, it will change your life and the way you look at life because my mother has definitely changed mine!

Sincerely,
Perry B. McClendon, Jr.

Foreword

When my Mom asked me to write the foreword for her book, I was a little nervous because I didn't know how and I was unsure about what to write. For a few days, I was very apprehensive about doing this but soon discovered the importance of it.

My mother's book is titled, *"In The Midst Of...."* It is a spiritual and well written poetic mastery that invokes the understandings of God's holy wisdom. I especially recommend this book to single mothers.

This book trails the teachings of Jesus. My mother then uses these verses and puts them into a story of her life. She is the greatest person in my life and is surely one of the most brilliant and gracious individuals I know. Her story is very gruesome and has many crests and troughs.

When my mother was divorced she was literally bruised in her heart! Although it was difficult, she proceeded on her journey to making it to the top. She held on and made it through. Now.....just look at where she is. She has grown so much in the Lord. She is so spiritual and I deeply admire that about her. She is truly my role model. She has set a good example for me and I want to be just like her.

My mother is truly my biggest fan and always will be. When you read this book, make sure to remember my mother in prayer. God bless you all.

Sincerely,
C. Taylor McClendon

Foreword

My name is Yvette Butcher. I am Theresa's friend and agent. I met Theresa about seven years ago at a youth football game, we've been friends every since. You might know us or have heard about us, we have been known to wear blue wigs to the football games! That's another story.

As you know, God has a way of making things happen, we were destined to be friends. If football was what it took then so be it. When we met, we were both sort of at one of those many forks in the roads of life as Robert Frost would say. Neither road looked as if it had been treaded and they were both going down hill, very steep hills.

Trust me God knows, He always knows. He knew we needed to be friends. He knew that both of us were living lives of quiet desperation. He knew we needed to be encouraged, inspired, lifted up, sometimes pushed and sometimes pulled. So it has been, we have played tug of war to ensure that the other would win.

Things have been rough. I don't mean to use that in past tense… things are rough. Money is tight but we have what we need, food is low but we have what we need, we don't like where we live but we have what we need, my car just gave up and Theresa's is on the last leg (rim) but we have what we need. You see, our faith is great. The scripture that comes to mind is Hebrews 11:1. "Now faith is the substance of things hoped for, the evidence of things not seen." Through it all we knew that TODAY was coming, through it all we had, NO, we have FAITH. You shall hear, Theresa's poetry truly reflects that faith.

It is my pleasure and my job to promote *"In The Midst Of"* and Theresa's future books. Now, Theresa, I am not trying to pressure you but you have a job to do, too. God has called you. Yes, the load is heavy, the responsibility mighty but if you couldn't do it, He would not have called you. Remember, I am not PRESSURING YOU.

Alright, you guys are in for a very special treat. I thank you from the bottom of my heart for sharing this first-time experience with Theresa. I invite you to sit back, open your heart and get ready to feel life…without further adieu, here she is my friend, my encourager, my Sister in Christ, Theresa Bailey McClendon.

Yvette K. Butcher
Friend/Sister/Agent

Foreword

I Peter 2:1-2 The Living Bible
To Jewish Christians driven out of Jerusalem and scattered.
Dear Friends, God the Father chose you long ago and knew you would become his children. And the Holy Spirit has been at work in your hearts cleansing you with the blood of Jesus Christ and making you to please Him. May God bless you richly and grant you increasing freedom from all anxiety and fear.

TBM's paraphrase:
To Theresa Bailey McClendon, who was forced out of her marriage and driven out of relationship with her local church, family, and friends and whose feelings were scattered about all over the city, the county, and the community.

Dear Theresa, God the Father chose you long ago, even before your birthday, and He has always known that you, Theresa, would become His daughter. And because he has always known this, He sent the Holy Spirit who has been at work in your heart cleansing you with the blood of Jesus Christ. He knows this will make you please the Father. So, because of this, may God the Father, bless you richly and grant you, Theresa, increasing FREEDOM from ALL anxiety and fear!

To this I say, "yes, amen, and alleluia!" Father, I do trust You, I will not be afraid of the pestilence by night nor by the arrow that flieth in the day. I will not fear man, for what can he do to me. I trust You. You know me. You created me. I believe that you have kept me thus far and I believe that You will keep me from now on. I truly, truly trust You. I give myself to you to care for me. You are my Mother and my Father.

I plead the blood of Jesus right now in my life, my sons lives, and on our circumstances. I break the curse of sin and death right now in Jesus' name, the name that is above all names. Thank you Jesus! I love and trust You!

From Your Heavenly Father!

FROM THE AUTHOR

My Name is Theresa, the Harvester

Strength under control is a beautiful thing. However, control over strength is detestable. This is a picture of a physically strong man or husband coming alongside his wife loving her as Christ loved the Church, until one day, the man becomes controlling and uses his strength, previously under control, to upset and abuse the woman and vice versa. The picture can also be found in any relationship, parent/child, child/parent, friend/friend/, sibling/sibling, church/parishioner you get the picture. This is not of God.

We were all put here for a specific purpose and when we allow the small 'g' gods to rule and super rule in our lives, we become frustrated beyond measure. Naturally, we won't find the increase in our lives that He promised.

To come back to the place of blessing
requires us to go through a time of testing.

Great times of testing require great preparation of strengthening or conditioning. It will be like making a decision to get your body in shape. The first step after the decision to get in shape is finding a gym and making application to join. When we decide to get stronger we in a sense make application to the God's Conditioning Gym! The hurt, the weak, the wounded, the sad, the depressed, the confused, etc. should be the first to apply! Make application quickly and discover your purpose in life. Discover what your name means and go do it! Mine means harvester.

Teaching
Hidden
Examples of
Righteous
Encouragement for the
Saints
Advancement!

Tendering
Hearts and
Encouraging
Restful
Excitement in the
Savior's
Affirming Love!

He is the Encourager!
I am Encouraged!
You be Encouraged!

I do believe that we all have at least one book in us, that is our testimony to why we exist. It was not chance that you haphazardly appeared on this earth, in your home, on your birthday, to the parents, you had under whatever circumstances…it was a plan!

And aren't you glad!! It was all a part of His plan to shape you and make you into the person you are and becoming! You, me, we are not accidents! And Father, how grateful I am that you have carefully knitted, down to the tiniest quirk in our personalities to bring you glory and to be an encouragement to one another! **Be encouraged!** *TBM*

DEDICATION

This year for Mother's Day, I already know what I am going to give. My book will be my Mother's Day gift to my mother, Mrs. Evelyn Mahaffey Bailey. I dedicate this Best Seller to you Momma! I cannot think of a greater honor at this time in my life. I have been searching for something to do, something to express to you how I feel and what you mean to me. Well, this is the best I have to offer, my testimony!

When my children speak of me, I know where they learned such warmth. Obviously from me and ultimately from you. I could only teach what I was taught. Thank you for your kind and careful treatment of me when I was a child. You taught me great manners even if I don't use them all the time. That's not your fault. Thank you for teaching me how to be gracious, sold out, and committed to whatever it is I'm doing. Your shoes are quite large so if I don't fill them up right now, at least I have hope! And Momma, thank you for modeling and teaching me a great work ethic. Amazing, you had nine kids during the 70's and 80's with very few problems. What a great testimony!

You were a stay at home Mom who cooked some fabulous down home meals. I can taste that sweet potato pie! I remember how you cooked at our birthday parties, collard greens, corn bread, fried chicken, the works! When kids would come and stay for dinner, you never sent them away! How I thank you for your generosity!

Teaching me to drive was quite a chore especially when you found out that I already knew how or at least I thought I did until you made me drive on I-85. I will never forget that and the lesson I learned that day when I ran over that dog. Wow! You were a brave lady with all those kids piled in the car! Thank you for convincing Daddy to let us take a friend on special outings, like nine children weren't already enough!

What a lady! You devoted yourself to one man and remained faithful! I deeply admired that! Whatever I can do for you is just not enough! Thank you Momma for modeling a faith in our Savior. I remember how we read the bible together and how you would read to me.....come to think of it, I miss that!

With great respect and gratitude, I love you!

Happy Mother's Day, Momma!

"It's mean and it's cruel, what's happened to me,"
said the butterfly
enduring all of the
squeezing, crushing, and pressuring
going on inside the cocoon!

"ONCE A CATERPILLAR BECOMES A BUTTERFLY, IT WILL NEVER CRAWL AGAIN!"

Second Corinthians 5:17 says, "If any man be in Christ, he is a new creature, behold all things are made new…."

The exact predicament of the caterpillar. It needed an *'in Christ'* situation, thus the cocoon and as a result, it became new, a beautiful butterfly. At any rate, the caterpillar was made new and it is further testimony to my icon, **"Once a caterpillar becomes a butterfly, it will never crawl again!"**

The caterpillar is one of God's most hated and unattractive creatures. We don't think twice about stepping on one and smashing it to its eternal damnation! We consider them filthy and grotesque to say the least. The thought of making a pet is a remote thought…however, this is how we are before we become…*'in Christ'*!

Becoming a butterfly is a process just as it is for us to become what God created us to become. We must be patient. The caterpillar is such a vivid example of the process of finding protection, nourishment, and nurturing when it goes into the cocoon. That's what happens when we are *'in Christ,'* we find protection, nourishment, and nurturing when we go into the church. The only problem is we are surrounded by so many imperfect examples. It's kind of like the eagle who dropped one of its eggs in a chicken's nest. After re-birth, the baby eagle found it difficult to fly while it was surrounded by so many chickens! He learned more chicken ways than he did eagle ways! Are you surrounded by chickens?

We, too, were unattractive creatures. There is a quote floating around Christendom that says, 'we are the only army that stomps our wounded!' What a horrific picture! I don't need to know your story, I have my own. It really doesn't matter if you're a major or minor part in your circumstances, there are those who think they have been born for such a time as this: 'to stomp you when you're down and make sure you slowly if ever get back up!'

Now that sounds awful, so deliberate but consciously, few people would dream of inflicting this kind of pain on others. But as the bumper sticker say, *'It happens!'*

"*In The Midst Of....*" is nothing more than my personal testimony of changing from a caterpillar to a butterfly. The purpose of it is to share and encourage others who are *'in the midst of'* their own circumstances, *'**you can make it**'* and come out much more beautiful than you ever imagined!

He loves me. I love me. I love you. Now who do you love?

IF you cannot get along, just go ahead and get *your* Divorce!

as if every couple had a divorce waiting to be claimed….

This, from a born again, bible thumping, scripture quoting, hymn singing, ………oh well!

I thought, if this is how a believer feels,

what hope is there for the unbeliever,

who has no hope in Jesus the Christ?

How sad.

This is such a mystery…….to me.

Sometimes it best to keep quiet.

"IN THE MIDST OF . . ."
"The Original Tree"

"And out of the ground the LORD God made to grow, every tree that is pleasant to the sight, and good for food; **the tree of life also in the midst of** *the garden, and the tree of knowledge of good and evil." Genesis 2:9*

That is how I see myself, as a tree. In fact, that is how I see women, as some forms of trees. Men in fact, I see as the trunks of those trees. God equipped them to be strong as well and to be a source of strength for themselves as well as the women they love. Children, I see as the branches of those trees. Ref. Psalms 128. They are the products of the relationship of the tree to the trunk.

There are trees that grow in clusters that are huge and their branches are heavy with some kind of fruit. Then there are trees that are alone with huge branches and great foliage that provide just the right amount of shade from summertime heat. Then there are trees that are small and seemingly insignificant that carry the sweetest fruit God has given us. There are also broken down, old looking trees that would seem to fair better if someone chopped them down but year in and year out they still hang on.

For me, this depicts the strengths and the weaknesses of women as well as men. Some of us have been through so many winters of hard living and yet our roots have continually gone down deep and our branches are now loaded with luscious fruit. Some have survived the great winters of their lives and lost most of their loved ones along the way and yet, they are still able to give soothing comforts of shade to those that are around them. In addition, some have just hung on by hook or by crook, with a determination that belies their appearance and produced some of the greatest people this World has ever known. These are single parent trees. Both men and women have done excellent jobs of maintaining homes as single parents. Then the broken down, old looking trees are those who have raised families on their own and yet still live and continue to raise grandchildren, great-grandchildren, nieces, nephews, etc. There are the young trees that are trying to bear fruit too early and quite often, they do not survive the harsh winters of life and they succumb to an early death. Sadly, these are young teenagers.

God has given us many, many trees in this beautiful place we call home and they all have a function. It is my desire to share with you, my function while here on earth.

As a tree planted here on God's green earth, I have begun to weather the storm. I can clearly see that the storm was not meant to destroy rather to cause my roots to go deep and find the surefooted strength of the Lord. The deeper we go, the greater our harvest.

I am thinking, *"when we go deep, a good harvest we will reap."* I once heard a preacher say, *"if you wish to walk on the water, you must get out of the boat."* Walking on water also presents the opportunity for getting wet. Going deep means we will have opportunities to get hurt. There is a digging in of the roots and breaking the hard, dry earth of the heart is not an easy task. *"But the deeper the root, the sweeter the fruit." Jeremiah 17:7-8.* Let your roots grow down into Christ and draw nourishment from Him. See that you go on growing in the Lord, and become strong and vigorous in the truth. *Colossians 2:7 The Living Bible*

Like so many trees before me, I did not decide to go deep; I simply decided not to give up. However, not giving up determined the depth of my destination. This was not a realization at the time, it just a matter of me making up my mind to **'try'** God.

As I watched natural trees survive the storms of their lives year in and year out, it occurred to me that something was keeping that tree. Rarely, do you see people out tending an individual tree. Yes, we have Forest Rangers who do an excellent job of preserving the forests and protecting the parks. However, I am speaking of the trees along the highways and byways of our lives. When great trees suddenly topple over and die, it amazes me and I always wonder *'who pushed it?!'*

As I studied Psalms One more closely, the Spirit of God began jumping up and down inside of me, I realized…that's me! That's me! I knew it was God. *This is my purpose*, He brought me out! My job is to share and encourage men and women so that they can see that He wants to make us <u>better</u> and not **bitter!** I am a woman and I speak from that perspective. Bottom line, the message is, He was keeping me, preserving me, and protecting me. **He** was and is the Forest Ranger of my life! In addition, like so many women and men trees that have gone on before me and will come on after me, **He** will keep them!

How blessed is the man who does not walk in the counsel of the wicked, Nor stand in the path of sinners, Nor sit in the seat of scoffers!

But his delight is in the law of the Lord, And in His law he meditates day and night.

And he will be like a tree {firmly} planted by streams of water, Which yields its fruit in its season, And its leaf does not wither; And in whatever he does, he prospers.

The wicked are not so, But they are like chaff which the wind drives away.

Therefore the wicked will not stand in the judgment, Nor sinners in the assembly of the righteous.

For the Lord knows the way of the righteous, But the way of the wicked will perish.
Psalms One

Amazing! I am thinking….Jesus was crucified on a cross that was made out of a tree. We are told to take up our cross and follow Jesus. Then God tells us we are blessed and will be 'like a tree'…. If this is true and I am sure that it is, then God is up to something. Because if there is a hope and any possibility that I might be like a tree then that would only mean that Jesus must be **'the original tree'**! His job was to come and show me how I could live. *Ref. Matthew 10:10.* "The Lord your God is <u>**in your midst**</u>, *A victorious warrior. He will exult over you with joy, He will be quiet in His love, He will rejoice over you with shouts of joy."* **Zephaniah 3:17 NLT**

While I am **'in the midst of'** something terrible, it takes a sheer determination of my will to be joyful. Amazing! His Word reminds me that **'in the midst of'** my circumstances, He is with me and He, Himself will rejoice over me.

Rejoice with me,
Theresa

"The Original Tree of Life!"

Your Love has changed my life and has taken me to a new height.
It is much more that I ever experienced, even as a wife.
Oh, you have not removed all of the strife;
Instead, you have given me a new lease on this life!

What a wonderful God who *gave* me His love
And if that was not enough He *gave* His Son from above.
The transformation continues like a hand being fitted for a glove.
Yes, the changes are tremendous – which I am very proud of.

It was You and You alone who believed what I could be
When I was really, so blind I could not see.
Because now I am planted by the waters like a strong oak tree
And marveling as I think it truly was *"Love that Lifted Me!"*

Yep! My branches are spreaded and heavy with fruit.
There is nothing more beautiful than spiritual loot!
Seeing others lives changed and wearing their strong suit,
Really makes me sad I let the adversary keep me mute.

But! I get over it quickly for there is much rejoicing to be done.
There are stories to be written, poems to be read and did I mention I'm writing a song?
Well as we continue the climb up Jacob's ladder and grab on to another rung.
It suddenly occurs to me, 'the battle is not over but as I remember, **we won**!'

Therefore, it is not preposterous that I think of myself as a tree
Especially since you yourself was crucified on **the original** at Calvary!
Because you knew in your infinite wisdom this is what I needed to set me free.
Hence, I sing at last, *"Oh how I Love Jesus because He First Loved Me!*

"Be Gentle With Theresa"
It's true,

I was stuck!

    I recognized where I came from and realized, I must move on. I refused to be
        self-defeating!

    I had made mistakes. *NEVERTHELESS,* I have punished myself, long enough.

    I had spent enough time comparing myself to myself,

To others
AND
reminding myself, "I DO NOT MEASURE UP!"

    Therefore,

1. Comparing old wounds;
2. Comparing present circumstances; as well as
3. Comparing healing processes

<u>No longer served me –</u> <u>IN ANY MANNER!</u>

It was time to move on.

<u>I was *HURT* the way I was **HURT!**</u>

I did what I did.
I am where I am.
There is nowhere else, I can be at this time in my life.

My circumstances and life experiences, unique to me, have brought me to this point and no matter where that is - or how it

Compares
with where anyone else is…

Now is the one and only starting point for

MY personal journey to FORGIVENESS and my ultimate FREEDOM!

" Be   Gentle   With   Theresa"

"Valley of Decision"

Multitudes, multitudes in the valley of decision! For the day of the Lord is near in the valley of decision. Joel 3:14 NASB

"Father, I want to know Thee, but my cowardly heart fears to give up its toys.

I cannot part with them without inward bleeding,
and I do not try to hide from Thee the terror of the parting. I come trembling,
but *I do come.*

Please root from my heart all of those things which I have cherished for so long and have become a very part of my living self;
so that
thou mayest enter and dwell therein without a rival.

Then shalt Thou make the place of Thy feet glorious.

Then shall my heart have no need of the sun to shine in it,
for
Thyself, the Son, wilt be the light of it, and

There shall be no night therein."

by Charles Swindoll,
Insight for Living Ministries

It has been said that Michelangelo could look at a piece of marble and receive a vision for that plain block of marble. This is what God does. He has been seeing things in us long before we are born. He not only sees us where we are;
He sees what we are to become!

"God Can Handle It!"

I worried over nothing! That's what Matthew 6:33 says. Satan would try to seduce me into feeling guilty and ashamed when I couldn't meet my monthly obligations. But I like what Liz Curtis Higgs says, "God is not shockable!" *"Really Bad Girls of the Bible."* And He isn't.

I wrote this piece after spending the whole weekend fretting over nothing! I didn't even owe what I thought I owed and I actually had a couple of dollars left over. When we stress over the small stuff it really grows into huge gargantuan size problems. But when we give it to God, He can handle it! For example, without spell check, there is no way I could spell gargantuan! I knew it started with a 'g' and an 'a' and I remembered there had to be an 'r'. After that I just threw in a couple of more consonants and ended it with another 'a'. I promise you spell check took it from there.

God says, you don't know it all, I am the spell checker, just give me your devotions, your prayers, your concerns, your thoughts, I've got this! Click under tools, click on spell check and watch me work! Small stuff, *"God Can Handle It!"*

"But seek ye first the kingdom of God, and his righteousness; and all these things shall be added unto you."
Matthew 6:33

"God Can Handle It!"

Be fruitful He exhorted and multiply.
Do this or else you will surely die!

Your fear of failure hides your gift.
Get down on your knees when you need a lift

It's the World around you who suffers the loss;
When you refuse to submit to the power of the cross.

The treasure is in the knowledge and the relationships skill.
And some is found in your experience or in your 'I will'.

Your obedience cannot be based on a child support check.
What if the mailman don't come, girl don't you fret!

You have spent too many years guarding the wrong treasure.
And when you open your eyes, you'll scream in pleasure!

I have an adventure for you, trust me it'll satisfy, it's enough.
You know I am a God of big things as well as the small stuff!

I see your anxiety. I see your long 'to do list'.
How many times do I need to tell you, don't worry, I've got this!

But because you think you know better, trying to be so smart.
You fail to do what I ask and that was to guard your heart!

You gotta trust me Theresa, I'm real! It's no trick.
I can't wait to hear you tell someone else, give it to my God, 'cause **He can handle it!**

If we succeed immediately, we don't learn anything.

"Waiting is Not Easy!"

When an eagle *(one of God's most magnificent creatures)* gets sick, it tucks its wings and soars, because eagles do not fly, to the highest mountain peak it can find. It allows the currents and the turbulence of the winds to carry it up, to the highest mountain peak it can find. Once it gets there, it lays itself out onto a rock and spreads those massive and beautiful wings of his. It just lies there for, as long it needs underneath the penetrating rays of the hot sun. He is allowing the rays of the sun to remove from him all of the infirmities or the sicknesses out of his worn body. When I first discovered this, it tickled me because the bible says:

"But they that wait upon the LORD shall renew their strength; they shall mount up with wings as eagles; they shall run, and not be weary; and they shall walk, and not faint." Isaiah 40:31 KJV

On the verge of becoming clinically depressed again, I failed to see how this verse applied to me. I was overwhelmed with the discovery that I was in the middle of a divorce. My whole world began to crumble. I could not fathom the thought of being single and with two boy children. I was devastated!

However, of all things God was calling me to WAIT! I thought how insensitive? Don't you realize what I am going through? Can you see? Do you see the funky debris of my heart? My sons heart? Don't you realize something needs to happen and happen quickly? Their lawyer is getting the upper hand!!!

However, He reminded me… Jesus **waited** until Lazarus died. *"These things said he: and after that he saith unto them, Our friend Lazarus sleepeth; but I go, that I may awake him out of sleep."* **John 11:11**

Like the eagle, it would do me, us well to fold our wings or rather lay down our day to day busy lives and mount up to the highest pinnacle in our hearts. That is when we find ourselves around the throne of grace, a high place of worship we need to lay quietly before Him. Sometimes we may lay prostrate before Him, other times, we may just kneel, and sometimes, we just sit. The important thing is to get before Him and allow the penetrating, soul-searching rays of the S-O-N to remove all sicknesses and infirmities from our tired, worn bodies.

Afterwards, He promised to renew us. I am glad that this is not just a one-time operation. It is for as many times as we need the surgery of the Word to cut away the meaty, fleshy thoughts and desires of our minds and bodies.

At the time of this writing, I am still going through a divorce but perhaps, just maybe, Lazarus has not died yet!?

He did promise!

"It Takes Strength To Do Nothing!"

                              I *Was* Hurt.

I was hurt!

I was hurt.

> ***Do this……***
> Take an unused envelope. Seal it. Press it firmly. Make sure the flap is sealed to the envelope. Now, take the envelope and lay it aside until you read this book in its entirety.

(Three months later!)

> Okay - you've read the book!
> Now. Open the envelope with your hand.
> Literally, rip the flap from the envelope. Do it! Rip it! All the way across the envelope until the two pieces are separated. Examine the envelope, examine the flap….there are pieces of the envelope on the flap and pieces of the flap on the envelope:

This is a picture of Divorce!

There will be a part of me on him and him on me, forever. However! Only God can heal the jagged edges of the rips of your heart! I am convinced that anytime there is a tearing away…of something that was once dear to you that it can and will leave holes in your heart, your esteem, and in your spirit. But God, is a restorer! And, He promised to restore to us the years that the locust did eat! Ref Joel 2:25.

I was on the phone with my friend, Edwina. She allowed me to cry, vent, scream, shout, and finally she would pray. "Tee, Tee, I hate you're having to go through this. I can hear the hurt. It must really hurt." Every time she said it hurt I wrote it down. I would write down parts of the conversation. *"I was Hurt"* is part of one of our longer conversations (and there were many).

Proverbs 27:17 is true, 'iron does sharpen iron.' I saw Ed as a strong woman and I would often tell her I wanted to be like her when I grow up! How wealthy I am to have Edwina Thierry in my life! How I wished Arkansas was across the street! Ed said on one occasion that she wished she could come feed me and we would sit up all night just talking! We are definitely planning that party, come on girls, let's do it! Mara, put it together, I'll be there! A hurt shared somehow does not hurt as bad. I was hurt but....

It does not hurt nearly as bad as it did.

I *Was* Hurt.

I was Hurt.
I was Hurt the way I was Hurt.
The Hurt was real and it really Hurt.
The Hurt was so real and intense; it left a hole in *my heart*.
The hole made more room for more Hurt to enter.
Hurt invited its old comrade, Bitterness. Bitterness was big. So the hole grew larger.
The hole was Unforgiving but Bitterness was welcomed. Hurt needed to increase.
So Hurt brought in a shovel called Anger.
Hurt used Anger to go deeper into Unforgiving, the hole in *my heart*.
Anger was very sharp and penetrating. Hurt was made stronger by Bitterness.
Finally, Anger struck gold and hit pay dirt, Resentment. Resentment stirred things up.
Hurt became addicted to Resentment.
Resentment was thrown into Unforgiving by its archenemy, Expectation.
Expectation only made Hurt realize just how bad it really Hurt.

BUT one day, Encouragement walked by and saw all of them lying around *my heart* drunk and worn out by the demands of Hurt.
After much inspecting, Encouragement began to *encourage* and *encourage* and *encourage* and *encourage* and *encourage* and *encourage* and *encourage*.

UNTIL, two years later, two ladies (twins) named Mercy and Grace moved in and began to clean up the debris around *my heart*.

<u>*Then*</u> my heart was healed and indeed made whole;
because
<u>Encouragement</u> is truly the lifeblood of the soul!

"Resentment is the cocaine of the emotions

Expectation is the mother of disappointment.

Bitterness is the reward of unforgiveness.

Anger is the fuel of resentment.

and

Mercy is the choice that makes them free and whole;

because

Encouragement truly is the lifeblood of the soul!"

I heard this in part from Chuck Swindoll, *Insight for Living*. When I heard it, it touched something in me so deep, so identifying, I knew there was a message for me.

Notice….I said I *was* hurt.

"The Metamorphosis of The Queen of Bitter!"

As usual, when the Lord generally inspires me to write, it was four a.m. I had had a particularly devastating night. The anger in my heart was so real and tangible. It had become such a part of me that I was uncomfortable not being angry. This particular morning I woke up in a daze. I really felt foolish. I had wasted another night of not sleeping.

I opened my bible to chapter 17 and chapter 42 from the book of Psalms, and everywhere I read, it seems I was being told to 'cry out'. None of this made any sense to me. Job responded by crying out to the Lord. He said, "I cannot keep from speaking, I must express my anguish. I must complain in my bitterness." *Job 7:11 NLT.* So I wasn't the first to be tell God how bitter I was.

Well there was nothing else to do but take God at His Word, so, I began to cry out. My first crying out was rehearsing my pain and my sorrow…before God, but somehow, after about thirty or forty minutes of that, it just seemed like enough was enough. I felt like I had God's attention, so why waste it continually complaining?! Not that God minds the complaining but for me, enough was enough. I was looking for answers and that's what drove me to my next step. So I prayed silently, I prayed conversationally. I prayed quietly. And then, I prayed loudly, out loud!

I began to pour myself out of myself. I began to confess and repent. I continued to confess and repent. By the time I realized what was going on, it was over! I was drenched in all kinds of bodily fluids. But I felt terrific! I was so excited, I began to write to try and capture this experience on paper, thus the birth of **The Metamorphosis**!

I must say, I love this poem. I call it my icon poem as it does capture where I have been to where I am and ultimately to where I am going. It says who Christ is, what He is doing, what He had done, and what He is going to do.

"The Metamorphosis of the Queen of Bitter"

Loud and long, the Queen would wail.
Daily rehearsing the past in great detail.

So much pain she could not stand;
All this brought on by the absence of her man?!

I think not! Her spirit prevailed.
Your soul is struggling between heaven and hell!

"What must I do?" came the weak reply.
Her voice was trembling like the beginning of a cry.

Walking towards her while she was so feeble and lost,
Was the very same One who died on **that** cross.

"Why Theresa, there's no need to fear anymore;
I was on my way to you at the first knock at my door.

Your heart has spoken much louder than your voice.
And I am here finally 'cause you've made the right choice."

So she gave up her throne where she was once Queen.
And quietly submitted to the now risen King!

Oh by the way, she's no longer known as the **'Queen of Bitter'**
NO, she's **better** because the King, He now lives in her!

"Nobody Else Can!"

Boy was I miserable! Poor Marilyn. I thought she prayed for me because I was a hopeless cause, she did and I was! I was such a mess! That's really why she prayed.

I know I had to be one of the most unorthodox clients she had. I would go in plop down on the couch screaming, kicking, crying, cursing, complaining until I was physically spent! Then I would go to sleep! I would wake up and there Marilyn sat eyes closed, hands folded, and praying out loud for me. I felt like a fool but then my emotions would take over and I would start all over again!

And to think, I would go sometimes twice a week! What a saint she is!

On this particular day, I was feeling sorry for myself…heck, no one else seemed to care! And I was lonely! I mean I was stuck on stupid! I complained that I didn't know how to do this, I couldn't do that, this was broke, that wouldn't work, the insurance was due, the check was short, this was turned off, that shouldn't be turned on, and on and on it went!

Peter asked the same question I did. When everyone seemed to have gone their separate ways, he asked Jesus, *"where do I go from here?"* REF JOHN 6:68

"Nobody Else Can!"

I felt so lost, so empty, and so very much alone.
The feelings come stronger especially when the kids are gone.

What do the lonely do and where do they go to play?
Do they sit like me and dread the night and waste away the day?

I cried and cried over again, feeling sorry for myself.
There was simply no one to love me to my right or to my left.

My counselor reassured me that Jesus is always there.
I adamantly responded, "I wished He would show me He cares.

Because nobody else loves me" as I gestured with my hand.
"Theresa," she gently whispered, **"nobody else can."**

"I wasn't the first person to ask the question 'where do I go?'

Peter asked it directly of Jesus. Jesus responded, "I love you."

I am so scared.
I fear being discovered.
I am terrified at these thoughts.

"What will people say?
What will they think?
What will they do?"

Why I look so good like a freshly made bed.
Why do I allow stupid thoughts to run through my pretty head?

If undeniably, there is no overflow
    Where indeed will the needy go?
What are we to think when life lacks such great compassion?
    Especially when love is measured with carefully, meager rations!

Even ***"In the Midst Of…."***

especially ***"In the Midst Of…."***

growing up ***"In the Midst of…."***

    fear and terror strikes at your heart ***"In the Midst Of…"***

"Most great men and women are not perfectly rounded in their personalities, but are instead people whose one driving enthusiasm is so great it makes their faults seem insignificant."

Charles A. Cerami
Author

"THE WASHING OF THE WATER WITH THE WORD!"

I sweated in places that were not lady like. I was covered with grime, dirt, and

God only knows what. I was tired, my hair needed washing and I am sure my teeth could use a brush or two.

I got in the shower and lathered up as my son says. I could not dismiss from my thoughts, 'the washing of the water with the Word.' Truthfully, to me, it did not make sense. How can plain old water make anything clean. Yeah, if you put something in it but not water alone, I just was not with it.

All of a sudden, it occurred to me. Eureka! **THE WASHING OF THE WATER WITH THE WORD!** The Word is the something, the cleansing agent, and the Water is rinsing, the freeing agent.

How neat!
How sweet!
How so much like Jesus!
I was excited. This is profound!
I love this teaching, it is solid and it is sound.
That would be Jesus. He deals with the practical
things in our lives……..
Mmmmm, he deals with the practical.

Consider Luke 7:36-50

You see there is a woman descried by others as a 'sinner'. Jesus saw something in her that no one else saw. Nothing is told of her sin, who she was, and where she had come from. Nothing.

But, I recognized her!
It was me!

~I can see the scene~

It was after a service. A special service or maybe it was just Friends and Family Day. Foods of all kind were brought in and served. A special table was set for the Pastor and his guests. Usually, a visiting minister or the associates but rarely a lowly individual with no claim to fame.

All of the best foods were reserved for the Pastor's table. And no one yes no one was allowed to sit without invitation. There was loud talk, inside jokes, and even a little flirting, but no ministering to anyone. All of that had been accomplished in the pulpit.

I stood and observed this knowing it really was the very last time.
For somehow I knew, this lifestyle would no longer be mine.

How often had I shared in what appeared a Holy Ghost 'good time'?
Father, forgive me for being ungrateful while drinking your holy wine!

The pushing and shoving to be noticed by the Pastor was such a sad sight.
I knew in my heart, my God was not pleased and that this was not right.

But something was missing in me, a very deep void.
I wished I had remembered to fill it up with You my Lord.

But I do not wish to be too hard - for with the same measure you mete.
Because to be invited at the Pastor's table was just quite a treat.

I cannot remember how, the occasion or the service.
The one thing I do remember is when I was invited, I was very nervous.

I looked down where I had just recently stood.
Thinking since I have arrived… why doesn't it feel good?

Then that's when I saw it, the loneliness and despair.
I knew what it looked like. Did I not tell you that I was just there?

I bowed my head, repented, and asked God to set me free.
May I never be willing to give to others what only belongs to thee.

I ate my food quickly and choked down every bite.
But somehow the delectables just did not taste right.

So, imagine my surprise after getting up from there,
Thinking, is there really a God and does He really care?

I read about *that* woman, *that* sinner, as the Pharisees described
Who could not gain acceptance no matter how hard she tried.

Her past was unyielding and would not let her go
Her constant torment must have been, 'I wonder do they know?'

Regardless of the sin, much too much energy is used removing the traces.
But remember God specialized in bringing strength at all the broken places.

Yeah, the oil was expensive. You cannot afford it if you have to ask.
Probably a few hundred dollars not including the flask.

To her it was nothing, she was just rehearsing the message in her ear,
When Jesus told John's followers, "go tell John what you saw and heard here."

Is it real? Could it be? Was it too good to be true?
Would this new teacher in town take the time for someone like me or you?

His presence, made me want to confess, 'I've been scheming and I've been lying!'

But when my eyes met His, I was overcome and started crying.

My tears were many providing so much water,
I was forced to use my hair to serve as a towel at this holy altar.

Imagine my surprise while kneeling at His feet,
That kissing and washing them would make me feel complete.

Then I broke open the oil and put it in His hair.
The cost again did not matter, I really did not care
.
~~~~~

Well I stepped under the water to finish my own shower
Allowing the natural water to wash off the dirt with all of its power.

Now, I do not know if you have sat here and understood what you heard
But to me, this is an example of **THE WASHING OF THE WATER WITH THE WORD!**

It really was cool! It was refreshing! It was a cleansing of my soul!
Especially when He said, "your sins are forgiven, go in peace, you've been made whole!"

So I did!

He knows…
He knew…
He has known.

I could not run…
I could not hide…
I will not pretend.

LISTEN!

<u>*He cares!*</u>

———

<u>*He leads!*</u>

<u>*He provides!*</u>

THEREFORE;

I will trust!
I will lean!
I will depend!

Life always goes forward NEVER backwards!

Lend Me Your Hope Lord!

Lord, I am down here doing life and nearly losing my mind.
Are you listening? If you are, would you lend me your Hope 'cause I am all out of mine!

Hope, as I see it is Faith with its clothes on.
But when I looked into my closet, I discovered I had none.

Now, I am tired of complaining, whining, and crying.
What I really need to know is if you will lend me your Hope, 'cause I am all out of mine?

Peter says that hope produces stuff in us that makes us not ashamed.
Well that's just life and its experiences, all going against the grain.

Now I'm not trying to be cute and I'm not just trying to rhyme'
I am only asking dear Father that you lend me your Hope, 'cause I am all out of mine!

Now, I cannot rest until I uncover exactly where my peace went.
What I really want to know is the *real source* of my discontentment.

Then I remember.... You said you would never leave me... no never alone.
That is why I know you will lend me your Hope! Because mine...it's definitely gone!

"Doctor Daddy!"

"He really needed stitches." That's what the doctor said. Man, that made me angry! "Don't worry" he said, "he'll be all right."

I know there is somebody who can identify with me! Us mothers get angry when somebody messes with our babies…we don't care who it is. Once again, gently, I heard the Master say, "do you think you feel any differently than me?" He always wait until I've done or said something stupid!

My own Dad used to say or do things that hurt me deeply. When I came to the Lord, I had a hard time transferring all of my trust over to Him or anybody. But what a time of testing there was for me when I realized that the events in my life were being orchestrated by Him! He was preparing me for major surgery, little did I know!

Today, I am grateful! The tears came and would not stop! But I am so glad He was there to cover and care for me! Our heavenly Father is so reliable. Me and my son are both all right!
He promised!

"Doctor Daddy"

My son cut his finger while hanging with his Dad.
The skin was hanging off, it looked pretty bad.

It was a horrible deep cut,
Something sharp went deep…sliced it right up!

He said it bled for awhile, it happened so quick.
I asked him if he cried, he said, "just a little bit."

As I applied medicine, I thought, 'this is what his Dad should have done.'
But perhaps responsibility would have interrupted their holiday fun.

I thought about my own father and when I needed help.
How often he told others when I thought, 'hey Dad, keep it to yourself!'

This tarnished my own belief about You, my heavenly Father.
I really couldn't understand when you said, "Theresa, just kneel at my altar."

I presented my wound to you - it was cut in my heart.
But You slowly and methodically applied 'your medicine' to every single part.

Oooh! It stings! It hurts! You see the cut went quite deep.
I thought You were being cruel - at least you could put me to sleep!

Like my son, I shed some tears except they were more like a flood.
The tears flowed even heavier when I realized the medicine was blood.

Eventually there was a soothing a dissipating of the pain.
It reminded me of the sign in the gym, 'no pain/no gain.'

Now that I'm all bandaged and feeling quite brand new;

I have a responsibility to tell others what You can do.

So when Daddy hurts you down here, don't fret and please don't cuss,
Just take your wounds to the Father 'cause He promised to take care of us!

"Me, Myself, and I"

I was beginning to sound like an old mystery movie, a regular old 'who dun it' special! The record was broke and I continued playing over and over again! After awhile, it really didn't matter 'who dun it' and or why they 'dun it'. Leave it alone. Let it be! Besides enough was simply enough!

I thought this was diplomatic of me and I deserved a reward, a pat on the back, maybe! However, once again, because I invited Him I'm sure, I felt the presence of the Holy Spirit speaking to me, *"Theresa, you are so full of yourself."* My first thought was to rebuke the devil and get those thoughts as far away as I possibly could. There is no way God could or would tell me I was self centered, not after all I had been through.

I do not intend to paint a picture of a harsh and cruel God, He is not! His heart is close to the brokenhearted, Psalms 34. And we are not always able to do 'the right thing and stop thinking about ourselves. It is a process over time. If you knock over a cup of milk, you can get up immediately and wipe it up but a baby will more than likely stand there and say something like, "uh oh...I made a boo boo!" But as he/she grows, she hopefully has been taught to immediately clean it up The bigger, the boo boo, the tougher the clean up but the process is the same, we must first admit to it. This is the beginning of taking the focus off of ourselves.

But the more I meditated on that thought, the more I realized, maybe He's a little bit right. In order to work through this thought, I had to remind myself constantly that God wanted nothing for me but good! I was simply too ashamed to admit I was selfish even to God. But once again, nothing shocked Him. All He wanted from me was for me to give Him glory, which He deserves.

Finally, I stepped out of **myself** and saw those other two imposters as well, '**me** and **I**. *That was a trio that could not carry a note and the group needed to be broken up.*

"It wouldn't be easy because they were in keen competition with another group named, '**You, Yourself**, and **You**' and both groups were fairly territorial and would not die easily. But once the rightful owner, Father, Son, and Holy Ghost took control. God got His glory.! Well, it's a much better picture as well as the music now that God is in control!

It's a good day to die!

"ME, MYSELF, and I"

Just when I thought it was others that made me hurt and cry,
Imagine my surprise when I discovered, it was **Me, Myself, & I.**

The bible declares that death was our last enemy that had to die.
But what a battle was fought subduing **Me, Myself, and I.**

Me was bold and highly favored,
Her stance was strong and deliciously savored.

There was no sharing with friends or even with her next of kin.
So **Myself** just stood up and boldly moved in!

And what a bold, impressive stance she took.
Never mind that she was perpetrating by hook or by crook.

But waiting in the balances was one much more imposing than either **Me or Myself**.
It was the baddest of them all, **I** tired easily, sitting high up on the shelf!

Words cannot describe the greatest of them all.
There are not enough expressions to paint a picture of **I's** gall.

Only her tongue could come close and recite her story so well.
Even then, you're left feeling empty without every detail.

She was as close to perfect as perfect could get.
And her life, she thought, was preferred by all that she met.

She was the object of envy and deep jealousy.
In fact, there were some that wished that *he* could be she!

Perhaps you're listening or reading this and wondering how could she be so crass.
Your answer can only be found by peering into your own looking glass.

Yikes! You must be shocked to see, it's not **Me, Myself, or I.**
Because *neither* of those three could ever make you cry.

So who is this imposter who looks too good to be true?
Look a little closer…it is **You, Yourself, and You!**

Oh no! It cannot be as you slowly begin to cry.
There are three of us in all of us who *really* need to die.

So with painful awareness you watch the death of your **Me, Myself, and I.**
And that's when you realize, it's not the first time you heard, "I think we should crucify."

It's funny to look back and see the strength of **Me, Myself, & I.**
But God was ultimately glorified and that was the reason why!

"Keep Your Eyes On the Cross!"

Circumstances hurt me so badly sometimes I could not only think, I literally could not see! I wanted so badly to be affirmed and to be told I was still liked! But somehow I just couldn't seem to get through to the right people. I just wanted someone to look at me appreciatively. Was that asking too much? Then I came across Job 29:24 in my daily reading. *"When they (Theresa) was discouraged, I smiled at them (her). My look of approval was precious to them (her). NLT*

God, you are awesome, You have truly thought of everything. I could always commune with you. I didn't necessarily need another person. I didn't need a man to affirm me but in due time you would send someone as long I remembered to 'keep my eyes focused on you!' With pleasure!

"Keep Your Eyes On the Cross!"

What a struggle it is for me, when I've had a hard day.
To bow before my Master and to kneel down and pray.

You and I both know that this is the way to go.
But my feet tend to follow my heart and they both are very slow.

It's my mouth that gives me the most problem, it runs so fast, ahead of my heart.
And it has the habit of speaking before I gather my thoughts!

Well I'm throwing another fit begging for someone to help me please.
But more and more the echo returns, "Theresa! Get down on your knees!"

My heart is so afraid - downright weak trembling with fear.
God, I know you're the answer but could a human wipe this tear?

What is it Father that frustrates me and makes me feel so lost?
My child, He gently whispers, ***"you took your eyes off the cross."***

"You Can Make It!"

"Come to Florida!"

"I don't have the $$$$."

"You get here 'T', I'll take care of you and get you back."

I hung up the phone. Diane was my big sister as she had called herself for years. I met her when I was in the military stationed in Athens, Greece. She is by far one of my dearest and best friends. She was a god send to me.

"Come" she said, "get some rest." It was Christmas time.

Shirley and I packed and hit the road. Shirley Caesar. She sang all the way, *"You Can Make It!"* I would sing with her when I wasn't crying. To this very day, I am convinced Pastor Caesar wrote this entire CD for me. I would say we worked it together but that would be lying.

You have to get a song in your heart. It has to be music that moves you, that inspires you, that gives you a hope. I am grateful for people who tolerated my singing. Often times, I would stop in mid sentence and start singing. I constantly reminded myself that I could and would make it!

"Thank you Pastor Caesar!"

"Thank you Diane!"

"Thank you Jesus!"

<u>*"I can make it!"*</u>

Dedicated to my sister friend, Diane Poole Thomas

"YOU CAN MAKE IT!"

…..sang Shirley Caesar

My healing vision.

I <u>choose</u> to heal!

I will no longer hold on to my grudges or resentments

Out of **<u>FEAR, ANGER, or PRIDE</u>…..**

I refuse to be intimidated **<u>any</u>** further
 by
The fear of being hurt again (I will test love again).
and
The fear of the Unknown!

Number two is an intricate part that will always
be a part of the Healing Process…
    It will always be present.

Number one however, can be conquered by creating
a vision of the destination I hope to reach….

The vision of the life I hope to lead and an image of the person I hope to become is a prerequisite for my healing. Thus:

"Once a caterpillar becomes a butterfly, it will never crawl again!"

"Unforgiveness is like drinking poison

and

watching the other person

waiting on them to die!"

Maybe to everyone else this is obvious, except to the person drinking the poison. We just don't 'get it'! The stronghold of unforgiveness has a magnetic pull that would challenge the gravitational pull of the earth's atmosphere!

The Protection of the Cocoon
"In the presence of the Lord, all I could do was cry...."

"The Glory Belongs to God!"

Some of the same people who are saying today, "girrrrlllll, you're a bad sistah" were saying I was an idiot yesterday! That's okay. People are fickle. And I am a people too! Only God is completely trustworthy. We're just commanded to be like Him, which means the longer we are with Him, and the older we grow in Him, we will began to look like Him!

Again, He's not shockable! Don't you love that about Him? I do! He knows our thoughts and He knows when we start getting a little big headed! The glory only belongs to God. Be careful though and remember Pete's admonishment. "Humble yourself….." I Peter 5:9. When we do, God will lift us up in His time! Yipppeee!

So, let's keep it real and admit where we are.

Holy Father,

Help me in my extreme weakness, I am nowhere near where I need to be but I am a long way from where I used to be. Thank you that You are not shocked by anything I say or do and help me when I shock myself. Thank you that in spite of me, you still bless me. Forgive me when I miss the mark and sin. Amen

"The Glory Belongs to God!"

I affirm myself mightily as I stand before the Lord
When I think of myself like He does, it's really not that hard!

It's hard to stay humble when you hear all day,
"girrrlll, that was so good! You have soooo much to say!"

Lord, I feel good right now, just staying in You; so don't let the praise go to my head!
But please don't leave me, you see I have not gotten out of bed!

You know what I need before my feet hit the floor.
You know what's waiting for me on the other side of that door!

Now I know your Word says You've already visited on tomorrow.
And I know you're not too happy when from the unknown, I borrow!

I just want to be do right and to my God be true.
I am not trying to take what only belongs to You!

So I see you're committed to my complete transformation
Your charge is still the same even for this generation.

My message to the saints must be simple and direct:
Peter says humble yourselves and keep yourself in check!

Get your bible off the shelf, especially when you're having a fit!
Open it up and read and believe all of it!

The more I read, the more I know.
The more I digest, the more I grow!

The problem isn't in the knowing, I just need to sit down and read.

And the problem isn't in the growing, I just need to plant a good seed!

I am to take up my cross, stop messing around, and faithfully tell my story.
And when I am finished, I'll sit down, and You'll get all the glory!

"True Confessions!"

Okaaaaaaay!

All the things I had been taught and had taught myself were thrown at me!
So why didn't it work? Whyyyyyyyyyy?
I see it!
They, the words, were thrown or vicariously delivered on the door step of my heart. There just seemed to be a huge shortage of people who either cared or understood.

What was I to do?

It was doing these times that I just learned to go before the Lord and just cry and pour my heart out to Him. I learned the cleansing power of tears. The best part was admitting and realizing His forgiveness!

"True Confessions!"

Words of wisdom thrown vicariously at the threshold of my heart,
Brought no more comfort than a love story written with slightly wet chalk!

Okay.... I know that this thought is senseless and thin as ice.
I just can't think of anything more ridiculous to describe Christians who aren't very nice.

Now don't be so snooty with your snide little self.
Come, try to understand me, bring your compassion, it's up on your top shelf.

Your words like mine, are wise - there's no question about that.
But must they be delivered with Sammy Sosa's hot bat?

My circumstances are strangling me, I can barely get out a cry.
And yet, I see you standing and glaring thinking you know the reason why.

Yeah, you think that I have sinned and done some awful thing.
Or else how could God allow me to have so much suffering?!

So, you're right He did say we would reap what we sow.
And Cloud and Townsend put it succinctly in their book on *"How People Grow."*

I know I cannot sow corn and expect to bring up peas.
But I can pray for crop failure, help me Lord Jesus please!

I've done so many things wrong and a very few right.
So it is with a repentant heart that I come to you tonight.

Forgive me for those times when I've thrown out words that were wise.
You see, I too, did not recognize Satan in his cunning disguise.

I am sorry when others came to me and I did not take more time.
I thought I was much too busy to stop on the proverbial thin dime.

And help me to remember, nothing is more important than a kindly spoken word.
And I must never forget that love isn't just an adjective, it's also a verb.

And may my life model yours so that the World may truly see.
That the good I do from now on is Christ working through me!

God's Riches At Christ's Expense!

"I have been crucified with Christ; and it is no longer I who live, but Christ lives in me; and the (life) which I now live in the flesh I live by faith in the Son of God, who loved me, and delivered Himself up for me." Galatians 2:20 NASB

I want my life to be an example of His poured out love on the cross for me ….

I was trying to cook while I was very upset. Generally, I've learned from counseling that your first thought is not the problem at all, rather it is a symptom of what's really going on. I found myself battling emotionally about the trials of separation, loneliness, children, and life in general. Depression consumed me…I was desperately focused on myself. I couldn't think, I couldn't perform, I was thoroughly depressed!

I spent at least two months of sleeping with my clothes on! That way, I didn't have to change when I woke up in the morning! Somehow I knew I deserved better. But how would I ever attain better. Unconsciously, I dumped a pile of salt into my pot. Whoops! I cursed! That's when it occurred to me that I needed balance. I was torn between my past and my future and I really did not know how to get over it. The present was killing me! I needed rest from all the torment I had put myself through!

I love acronyms. To me it's exciting to take a word and actually define the meaning of that word or further clarify it by adding on new words. **GRACE!** It was the finished work of Jesus on the Cross of Calvary: **G**.od's **R**.iches **A**.t **C**.hrist's **E**.xpense just made sense. I realized I would never be able to pull this off without Christ. It had to be Him working through me… Him pouring into me makes me a salty offering to Him!

"God's Riches At Christ's Expenses"

One day while cooking I picked up a box of salt.
Amazing I need this so my food doesn't taste like chalk.

However, if I use too much, it will taste even worse.
Too much too little – I cannot decide so I curse.

What is the issue at hand I hear the voice in my heart?
What has caused so much trauma that I do not know where to start.

Yeah, the acronym says '**G**od's **R**iches **A**t **C**hrist's **E**xpense';
More often, it's used to justify my seat on the fence.

Balance! I hear the word screaming to be embraced.
That is the whole point of His *Amazing* **G. R. A. C. E.**

Get down- get off and get on with your living.
Don't you realize you have already been forgiven?

You no longer need salt to make your life sweet.
You only need to remember the scars in my hands as well as in my feet!

Follow after me and I will make your life complete.
In addition, dreams will come true even while you are asleep.

Now your sleep will not be natural – it is a spiritual, power nap.
And that my child is a Holy Ghost wrap!

"The Leper's Song"

Lord, I was so unattractive. I moaned, groaned, and complained until I made myself sick. What's worse, I surrounded myself with others who moaned, groaned, and complained as much I did. I was a leper...no one wanted to be around me....I didn't even want to be around myself! However, one day, as James Cleveland would say, "my faith looked up!" When I looked up, I saw Jesus and I begged Him to have mercy on me.

Consider Luke 17:11-19

And it came about while He was on the way to Jerusalem, that He was passing between Samaria and Galilee.

And as He entered a certain village, ten leprous men who stood at a distance met Him;

and they raised their voices, saying, "Jesus, Master, have mercy on us!"

And when He saw them, He said to them, "Go and show yourselves to the priests." And it came about that as they were going, they were cleansed.

Now one of them, when he saw that he had been healed, turned back, glorifying God with a loud voice,

and he fell on his face at His feet, giving thanks to Him. And he was a Samaritan.

And Jesus answered and said, "Were there not ten cleansed? But the nine-- where are they?

"Was no one found who turned back to give glory to God, except this foreigner?"

And He said to him, "Rise, and go your way; your faith has made you well."

I do not know where the others are; I can only speak for myself. I am grateful and a grateful heart must sing. Therefore, I sing, **"The Leper's Song"** with joyful enthusiasm!

"The Leper's Song"

Thank you Lord for . . .

NOT - killing me while I was *in the midst of* my sin; but for
GIVING- me another opportunity to show that Christ lives within.

NOT- deserting me in my deepest hour of need; but for
GIVING- me just enough and not entertaining my greed.

NOT- condemning me when I looked at others with pride and contempt; but for
GIVING- me the courage to confess that I really was a wimp.

NOT- consuming me in your anger when I didn't walk in your will; but for
GIVING- me friends who held me accountable and said, "Theresa, girl, just be still!"

NOT-so much as what you have and what you have to give; but for
GIVING- me Jesus and the opportunity to have life and   really begin to live.

So it is . . .

NOT- for the gifts that makes life less hard; but for the
GIVING- like the leper I say, "Alleluia, thank you God!"

"Who Told You Were Naked!"

Everybody knows! You could not convince me that everybody knew the pain in my heart. Boy was I out of it! Pain, unbalanced, makes us think too highly or not enough of ourselves. But the truth be told, I felt naked! Isn't that the way Adam and Eve felt in the garden, but you say, they sinned. Well so did I and you did too!

Nevertheless, God, killed enough animals to clothe them. Just the same, He killed His Son Jesus so that He could clothe us in His righteousness. I am covered in precious blood! Whoo oo! Makes me wanna jump up and down!

And get this....nasty as we are, God still desires intimacy with us. This really gets me going, I keep trying to hide. This is a direct missile from Satan called guilt and shame, designed only to keep me hidden. There is nothing He doesn't own and nowhere we can go that He does not know already where it's going to lead. It would be hard trying to play a game of hide and seek with God, don't you think?

Dear Father, I am glad you persisted in seeking me out, I really feel good about that. Thank you.

"Who Told You - You Were Naked?!"

I heard you coming, so I hid.
I was afraid you'd find out what I did.

My heart was quite tender and very much exposed.
I was quite embarrassed for you see, I had on no clothes.

I walked around with my head hanging down.
It was too much like work to do anything but frown.

I recognized this feeling – it was not new to me.
It's primary purpose was to keep me from being free.

I heard you coming, so I hid.
I was afraid you'd find out what I did.

It stalked me. It haunted me. It made so ashamed.
There were times I tell you – I couldn't remember my name.

"Come closer," He called in the cool of the day.
"I desire to be with you – I have something to say."

My heart still tender and now quite exposed.
It forced me to confess – I had on no clothes!

I heard you coming, so I hid.
I was afraid you'd find out what I did.

I was afraid of this moment, I knew it was sacred.
So I reluctantly admitted, yes, I am naked.

"Who told you you're naked – have you eaten of the fruit?
Have you listened to those lies and rejected my truth?

I love you my child – come closer to me.
With you I desire complete intimacy."

I heard you coming, so I hid.
I was afraid you'd find out what I did.

I hesitated. I came. Then my feet picked up speed.
My heart was determined to get past my deed.

He's calling me. He's beckoning in that still, small voice.
"You're not bound to your past – you now have a choice.

I threw off all hesitation, I had to draw near,
I was determined to no longer be controlled by timidity and fear.

I heard you coming, so I hid.
I was afraid you'd find out what I did.

I will clothe you in my righteousness. I'll clothe you with care.
Don't listen to the enemy, no matter what the dare.

Come out into the open. Come receive of my love.
I have covered your entire life with my Son's precious blood.

You are now an ambassador sent for others to be free.
Your nakedness is covered and you can thank *Calvary*!"

I heard you coming, so I came.
~*Selah*~

"Living Well"

A honey bee darted from bloom to bloom
    Looking for a flower to make honey, very soon.

The touch must be perfect, not too hard not too light,
    Always ready to lift up and take flight.

Where is the beauty in a bee and a flower?
    The bee is only looking for a honey of a shower!

Aha! The beauty is in the giving from sweetness of the root.
    The flower actually lives to produce more fruit.

After it gives, it closes its bloom and it will finally die.
    What a strange thing. I can hear you asking, "I wonder why."

The flower did not exist to live forever, no its purpose in life
    was to eventually move on.
What's important though, is not why it was here rather what it
    left after it's gone.

So live your life and make you sure you live it well.
    Then few will ponder when you die whether you went to Heaven or whether you went to Hell!

Questions - Answers

When I study the book of Job….there are all kinds of emotions going on with this poor man! Why, one might ask would God allow such tragedy. Well we're all pretty certain after we read the entire book of Job. But it's that 'in the midst of….' that causes us so much anxiety! No matter how much you think you know, God knows best and some things He just does not need us to know the answers to right now. That's all right with me, what about you?

Questions - Answers

Can conversation like love be nurtured and cultivated?
How is it possible to love You and hate what You created?

Is it possible to desire Your peace and reject Your living Word?
Can a sentence be formed without having a verb?

Can a bird lay an egg without having a nest?
Can a gorilla be proud without beating his chest?

How can you hate the one who said, "I do?"
And when the same person sneezes, "you say, God bless you!?"

Why do good people die when they are so young;
And the really mean ones seem to always hang on?

Are there questions in life for which there is no answer?
Did you hear, I think some guy found a cure for cancer?

Why is failure so vital to any success?
And can a degree be obtained without passing a test?

Who turns off the stars and pulls down the night shades?
Whose idea was it to create the Florida Everglades?

Why is it some kids live in such miserable homes?
And what did we ever do before we had cell phones?

Who knows how many grains of sand are on the beach?
Here's my favorite….do teachers know the answers to the things they teach?

Is it called a language when you groan and moan?
Is it only old people who get cold in their bones?

I don't know the answers to very many things.
Especially when I see teenagers' noses with tiny, little rings!

But to all our questions from A to Z, including all kinds of cancer;
Me, I don't have a clue, but I do know, deep in my heart, Jesus is the answer!

F R E E D O M

(From a previously caged bird!)

Paul Laurence Dunbar declared, 'he knew what the

caged bird sang and he knew why the caged bird sang!

I would imagined he knew that among many other things!

Maya Angelou declared that she knew why the caged bird sings!

I imagine *you* know why the caged bird sings!

But I want to express why this caged bird could not sing!

Your blessings exceed my wildest imaginations!
 <u>Thank you and I love you Lord!</u>

Alleluia!

No longer caged.

"Why This Caged Bird Could Not Sing!"

It's a mystery to the average man,
The simple ones just can't understand!
The learned ones find it hard to believe;
And the magician thinks the answer is up his sleeve!

What is it? How is it? What's the great mystery?
Aw Lord, my God, they can't hear this from me!
You must relate the answer and be precise to a 't';
Just tell them quite simply, this caged bird could not sing because he was not free!

But wait! There's a hum, I recognize that tune…
It's the once caged bird singing, *"Soon and Very Soon!"*
Hey! He died for me! My voice, I will not waste!
If rocks can rejoice and birds can sing, I should be praising God all over this place!

He broke down the barriers, He tore down the walls!
He totally gives me His Grace doing away with old laws.
I was beat down it's true, I once was caged.
But I'm so much improved, I've gotten better with age!

This Love is real, it's personal to me.
I serve a God who died, willingly!
"And I sing because I'm happy! And I sing because I'm free!
His eye is on the sparrow and He watches over *T*!"

My Favorite Songs

"Amazing! The song says of Grace."

"Jesus loves me this I know for the Bible tells me so."

Sounds like

Roses are red - violets are blue.
Usually means someone loves you.

*"Little ones to Him belong,
They are weak but He is strong."*

Roses aren't always red and violets may not be blue
But I am certain Jesus loves me and He is faithful and true.

*"Yes! Jesus loves me. Yes! Jesus loves me!
Yes! Jesus loves me. For the bible tells me so!"*

That's why I sing:

*"Oh! How I love Jesus!
Oh! How I love Jesus!
Oh! How I love Jesus! Because He first loved me!"*

"Amazing! The song says of Grace."

"My First Choice!"

I Gotta Tell You, There's Some More Hurt!

I told you it hurt too much to share.
I clearly understand that I am to keep my face and faith looking up!
North is always up! And besides, there are some things you should only tell God.

He knows!

"The mouth keeps silent to hear the heart speak."
Alfred De Musset 1810-1857

You have thoughts that could be recorded here:

"My First Choice!"

I Gotta Tell You, There's Some More Hurt!

Something else hurts.

Something happened yesterday that just blew me away.
It hurt my heart so bad, I didn't know what to say.

*I drove around like a Zombie looking for someone to share my load
I arrived to my destination safely, I traveled in automatic mode.*

*Just when I thought I had arrived;
Just when I thought I could survive;
Just when I thought I had been revived;
Something happened and I almost died!*

What could go so wrong in such a short time?
What could possibly cause my heart to fail?
What on earth would make me cry?

Lord…..I thought I'd seen it all, I started to murmur
But before I could get started, "Stop it!" He said,
"You are an Overcomer!

This was to try you…you see, it's a test
I wanted you to see that you need Me at your best!

Theresa, 'don't take your eyes off the cross' remember that's what you wrote.
You're one of my chosen sheep, now stop acting like a goat!

For the first time in your life, you didn't go and cry to someone.
And you really came running when you heard me say, 'come!'

Okay some are blind and can't see your gift flow…
My child, keep your focus on me and learn to say, '**SO!**'

They didn't call you, they didn't give you strength.
Turn your face to the North, for freedom that's where your people went!

And remember from now on, as you continue in your purpose and on your life's path.
Always, always make me your first choice and never the last!"

"There's Nothing More Exciting Than A Strong Woman!"

I am not weak.
I am not weak.
I am not weak.
<u>I am not weak</u>!

I had to learn to speak to myself like I am the woman that God created me to be. The more I spoke it, the stronger I became.

Many women asked me if I could write something for them. I never sat down to write this book, I was only journaling. It was my way of healing. I had done this for years. However, *I opened my eyes to the hurts and pains of other women around me.* As I ministered out, God ministered in. I saw where I had come from, I saw where I had been. I saw where I eventually wanted to go but most of all, I saw other women.

Many were feeling hopeless, living defeated, flopping hopelessly, and most were just existing. But as I looked closer, I saw strength peeking through weakness. It was amazing! I had to look a little closer. I actually saw my own strength by looking at their strength. Many would say to me, "oh Theresa, you're so strong!" I begged to differ. But I was, God made me strong.

There was some strength coming through. Oh Lord, show me how to help another see what you have put in them. Even though I am still going through the 'valley of the shadow....' To others I appeared to be stronger and the reason why is because I am!

Who showed me?
Incredible! Eureka!

There were others who had traveled the road that I was on. I realized I have a conscious responsibility to share with other women. God made sense of my hurt...my purpose is to share my testimony! This is exciting! Even more exciting is watching and listening to the responses of women when I shared it with them.

This piece is dedicated to a couple of women in particular but in actuality, it is for every woman in general. Mara, are you there? <u>Hannah, you're stronger than you think!</u>

"Who is weak without my feeling that weakness?"
2 Corinthians 11:29a NLT

"There's Simply **Nothing**
More Exciting
Than
A Strong Woman!"

"There's Nothing More Exciting Than A Strong Woman!"

She does not need identifying.
She just knows who she is - there is simply no denying!

It does not matter the color of her God given skin.
Her strength comes through regardless of who she is and where she has been!

Her smile may be exposed through crooked teeth, straight, or covered with braces.
However, her heart exposes evidence of God's healing at all the broken places!

What is her secret? Where does her strength come from?
From her heritage? From her mother? Some colleague? Some chum?

She is not always this strong - there are some days when she does not look good.
That would be superficial, not real at all and really ..... nobody should!

She has had her moments when she looked a little beat down and not so together.
She would cry at the wrong time and worried if she would ever be any better.

There were some days when it was hard just getting one leg out of bed;
But the greatest trial came in getting the nonsense of her head!

She would take a minute to cry and it turned into a week,
She would take a moment to reflect and her future seemed bleak!

What should I do? Where should I go? I hear the questions being formed.
Girl! Get up! Gather your strength - it's time to move on!

Move on! Come on …. to higher and better ground.
<u>FORGET</u> the voices in your head and ***don't you dare*** turn around!

There are sisters who are waiting for they have been there too!
With strength like elephants, they are waiting to encourage you.

The tears may continue but straightened up your back.
You have everything you need - there is simply no lack!

Just be a good student and learn your lesson well.
For in a few short years, this same story, to others you must tell!

"There's *Simply* **Nothing**
More Exciting
Than
A
Strong
Woman!"

"Clay Feet In High Heels!"

The book of Daniel, the second chapter makes reference to a huge and powerful statue of a man shining brilliantly, frightening, and awesome. He described it beautifully from the head to its legs. He was made of gold at the head, silver on the chest, all kinds of precious metals until it came to his feet. They were made of clay. But a rock (Jesus) smashed the mighty statue (Theresa) and the rock that knocked down the statue became a great mountain that shooked the whole earth.

This is written in remembrance of my being carjacked. There were many other things happening to me at this time. I was devastated at the viciousness of the rumors. I was in a horrible situation, I felt I had nowhere to turn. Life was requiring way too much energy. It was not supposed to be this way. I could not take it anymore and I needed to get my weak clay feet out of those high heels! Only Jesus was willing to touch my feet and subsequently touch my heart!

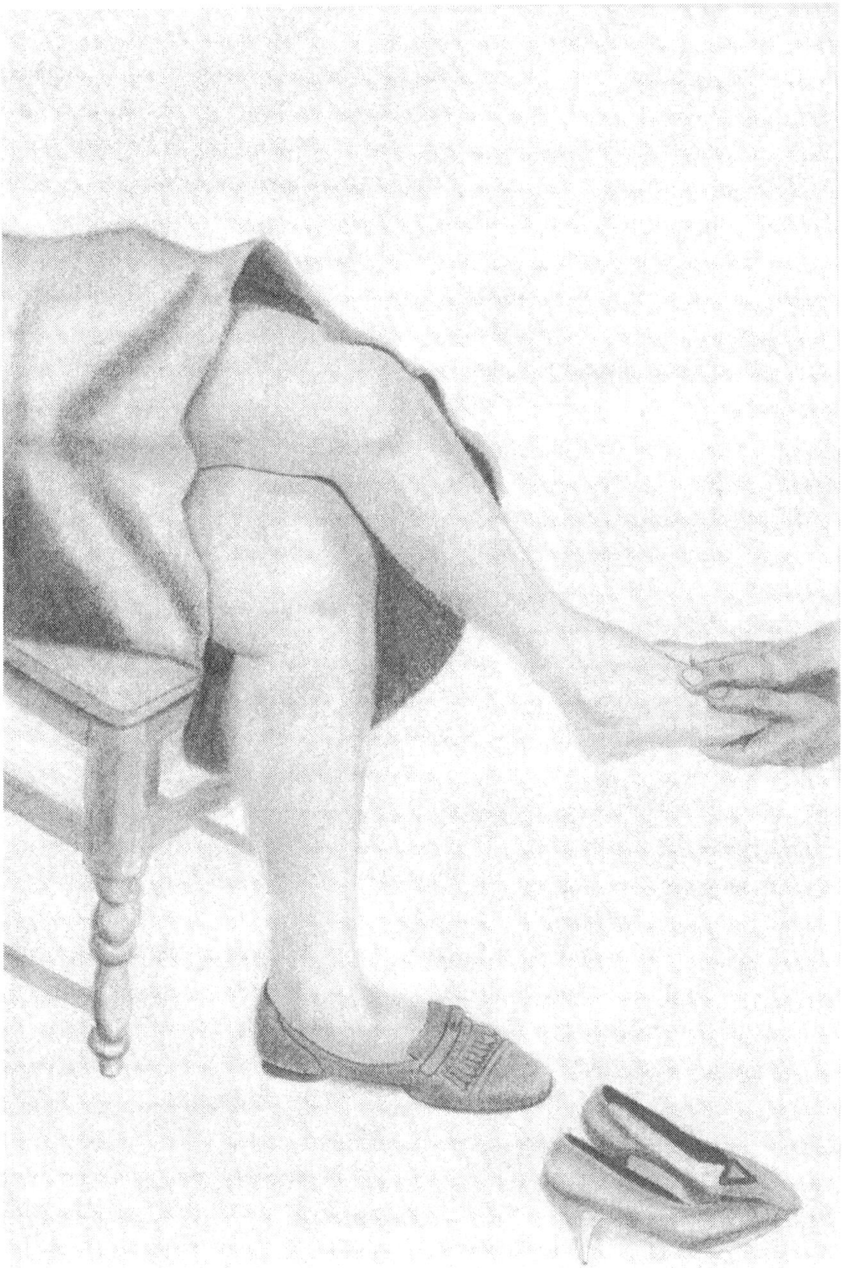

"Clay Feet In High Heels!"

My tank is running low. I see the gauge on *'E'* which means Enough!
Enough of the abuse, enough of mistreatment and all of the other stuff!
Enough of religious traditions, the World and all of its frills.
I am just a tired, old woman whose ***clay feet hurt in these high heels!***

My past stalks me like the kids who carjacked me in the parking lot.
They moved quietly and effectively as criminals usually do in the dark.
They seemed oblivious to my screams and even less to my tears.
They probably knew I was a tired, old woman whose ***clay feet hurt in high heels.***

I was even more devastated when people said the fault was all mine.
They said I was in the wrong place, with the wrong people, at the wrong time.
The gossip coupled with the attack gave my soul horrific chills.
I thought, 'who would hurt a tired, old woman with ***clay feet in high heels?'***

But wait! I am young and vibrant and oh so full of life!
Yes, I had been beat down badly both as a friend and as a wife.
My days were consumed with any number of pain pills
It was no wonder my ***clay feet hurt in those high heels.***

Galatians 2:20 says it is Christ who does the work, not I.
The truth was so revealing, I did not even take the time to cry.
Determined to move forward and yes to do God's will,
I watched as he tenderly lifted a ***clay foot that had been in a high heel.***

He massaged my feet and they both were relieved.
His touch was so powerful; it touched my heart where I had grieved.
Now I am wearing comfortable shoes and ready to enjoy life and its many thrills.
What a joy! What a relief to no longer have my ***clay feet in high heels!***

"It is Well!"

I'm still wondering what do I say…
When people ask, "how are you doing and how is your day?"

Do I smile? Do I lie? Do I say, "everything's all right?!"
Even though it ties my tongue and causes my heart and head to fight.

I know the heart controls the emotions and how you really feel.
But a fight is guaranteed because the head insists on 'keeping it real.'

Forget your being whiny.   Forget your being real.
Why can't we just be honest and tell it like it is.

My wallet and my heart are both very broke.
And my faith is being challenged like two hands around my throat!

I have the tendency to whine when I should lift up a praise,
I know that is the process, I'm just going through a phase.

But my God is so generous, His mercies are new each day
And he chooses to minister to me in His own unique way.

I began to meditate and think on how far I've come;
To me it looks like I've been crawling, to others, it looks like a run!

True! I had been through some things but God just opened my eyes!
This was all a part of His plan, this really was no surprise!

He has provided in every way plus a roof over my head.
And what a testimony I have…. even about my bed!

So you see when others ask, I don't dare share every detail;
I simply answer like the Shulamite woman, "my friend *it is well.*"

"On My Knees"

Ultimately, "*On My Knees*" is written to my Lord. However, He did put us here for the ministry of 'one another' as well. Let's see what Job has to say. From *Job 6:14*:

To him that is ready to faint kindness [should be showed] from his friend; Even to him that forsaketh the fear of the Almighty. KJV

A despairing man should have the devotion of his friends, even though he forsakes the fear of the Almighty. NIV

One should be kind to a fainting friend,, but you have accused me without the slightest fear of the Almighty. NLT

To him who is about to faint and despair, kindness is due from his friend, lest he forsake the fear of the Almighty. AMP

Theresa Bailey McClendon was about ready to give up, throw in the towel, quit life, and she needed the devotion, the kindness, the commitment from loyal friends and believers who had a deep reverence or respect for El Shaddai or the Almighty God. TBM

Take your pick. This poem without reservation is dedicated to the many, many new friends that I made after my new way of life began. (I did not keep custody of my old life. The fight was too great and my energies were needed for me and my sons, whom I did keep custody of.) For me, this was a moment of choosing my battles and this was not one I cared to fight, it was too heart wrenching.

One new lady friend in particular comes to mind. Her friendship is one that I treasured immensely, not above any others, she and I just shared some deep personal conversations that shall forever remain with me and God. Her name is Andrea Skinner affectionately known as 'Andy'.

When I shared my story with Skinner as I called her, she very bravely declared that she would be my sister. And thus we were, sisters from another mother! Well Skinner moved from Norcross, Georgia to her eternal dwelling place and what a sad day that was for the folks in Norcross. But heaven on the other hand was having one huge *'Welcome Home Party'* I'm sure!

Thank you Lord for people like Andrea Skinner! *What would I have done if I had never found her, I wonder out loud 'cause I'm not too proud…..*

With great love and affection, I dedicate, "On My Knees" and "Sisters From Another Mother!" to the sweet memory of Mrs. Andrea Skinner.

"On My Knees"

What would I do if I'd never found You?
I wonder out loud 'cause I am not too proud.

You are my refreshment like the dew of the morning
after a hard rain.
You are the One that keeps my heart from being manhandled by my brain!

I love You! I need You! I really must confess!
And it's not because You are the only One who can get me out of this mess.

No! You see, You are my light in darkness…
You are my ship on deep seas.
And it is more than my privilege to honor You
on my knees.

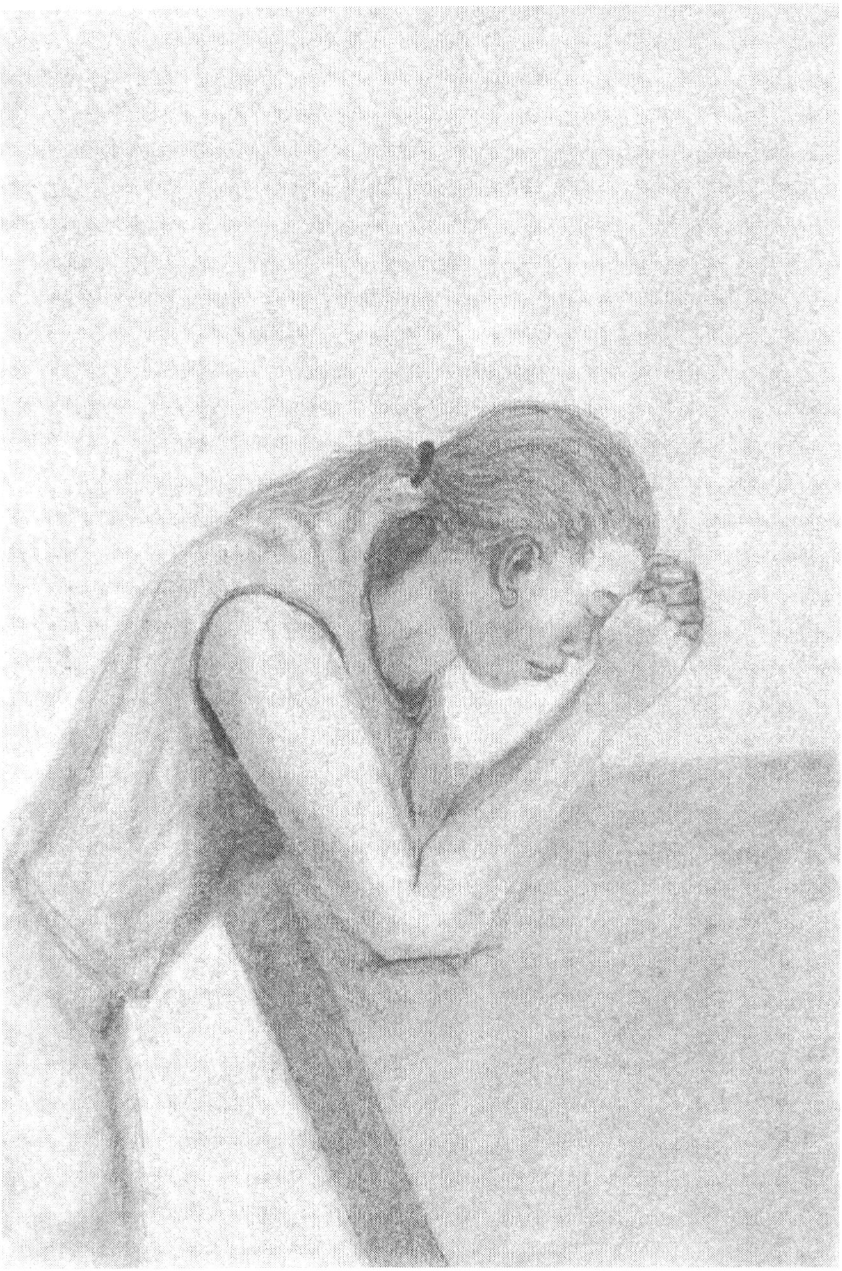

"Sisters From Another Mother!"
(Bits 'n Pieces of a Conversation)

"Hey Youuuu!
How're ya feelin'?
PHAT, black, and happy!
Youuuu?!
PHAT, white, and happy!"

'Thank you and I promise to pledge to call if I'm in trouble.
You call me, I'll make you smile, my sister from another mother!'

You know we share a love of a Savior who died to make us brothers.
"Didn't we do the same thing when we both became mothers?!

I only say such crazy things when it's you I'm talking to."
'Yeah, blame it on me for exposing the crazy in you!'

"It's really cool the way we relate and can talk to each other."
'I glad God sent you, I love him for that, my sister from another mother.

Andrea, you take every day as God gives it to you.
It always involves helping others…it's amazing what you do!

You give your life to God such a sweet offering
I wonder if you're like me, do you have any suffering?

Well let me encourage you, you see that's what I do
It'll be my personal pleasure to give something back to you!

To encourage means to strengthen, to inspire and to cheer
Already the table has been turned around you're sending an email here!

I am supposed to be the one to do this for you
And then I get this email saying, 'open when you're blue!'

Just give me a minute, I'm coming out of this chair…'
"Don't rush it Theresa, you'll give me a scare!"'

Listen Skinner, I'm thinking of you today saying a prayer, girl, do take heart.
Gather your strength, be inspired, and let today be a fresh start!

"I get it my friend." Andy jumped in, "we'll be there for each other."
'You got it girl, always forever, <u>sisters from another mother</u>!'

God's Word

<u>*Will*</u>

Disturb the Comfortable,

And

Comfort the Disturbed!

There were times I tell you when I could be found on both sides of these statements. Today I can identify with those who are on either side. This has given me a greater sense of compassion for either group and today, I can agree with my brother, James who says to count it all joy when you're going through various trials…..chapter one, verse two.

The people who are the most unlovable, are the ones who need love the most!

Look around	-	*you'll be distressed.*
Look within	-	*you'll be depressed.*
Look to Jesus	-	*you'll be at rest.*

Live the remainder of your life as the best!

Dear Father,
Thank you for what you've done for me. Thank you for the metamorphic change in me. May my service to others bless you. I will never be the same again to your glory. Thank you for teaching me that Faith always looks up and never within and definitely not around. Amen.

"The Touch"

I'm a people watcher… I especially enjoy watching couples. It's interesting to watch and see if I can tell if they are newly weds or old timers.

I enjoy a good chick flick every now and again. I am convinced they make those movies for die hard romantics like myself. In the movie I have in my mind, the wife has caught the husband in an adulterous position. She calls him on the carpet and he gets burned!

The consequences are tremendous. He loses immediate fellowship with her, their daughter, and her family. After she displays the courage to call him out, her mother finds the courage to call out her husband. It is a romantic comedy of sorts except the offenses are not funny.

However, both men found themselves wooing for the attentions of their wives. The older couple did not take as long to make amends. The younger couple was another story which is why I gave up a precious $5.00 to own this movie! The man furiously courted his wife! He really wanted her back! He was deeply remorseful over his offense. She, however, was unrelenting and made him prove that he could be trustworthy! He had no problem. He was patient, focused, and very, very kind. I almost wrote a letter offering him my hand!

I enjoyed this movie as you can tell. It caused me to long for 'the touch' of a sweet and loving man. All I can say is I have made up my mind to not compromise my values and God comes along and gives me His strength through His touch. For that, I am grateful.

Mmmmmmmmmmm……. *The Touch.….*

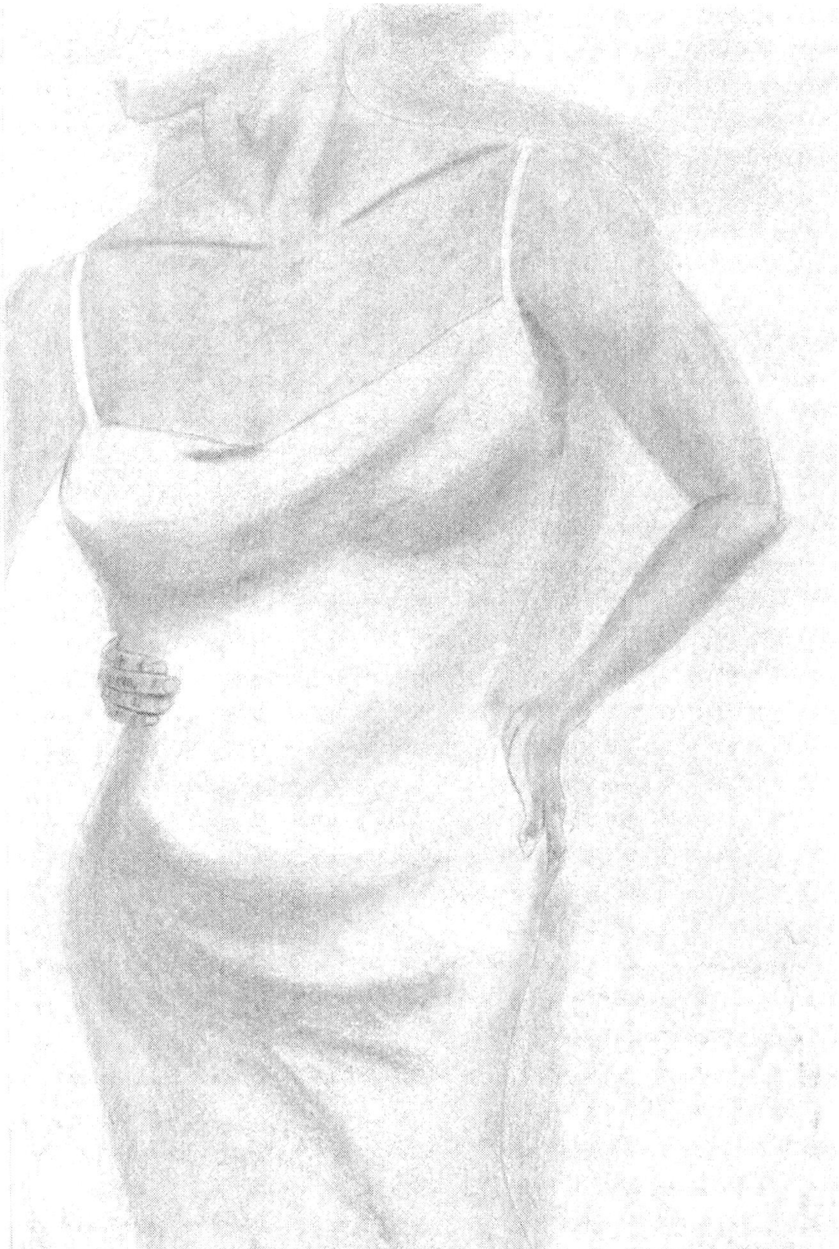

"The Touch"

What must it be like to have **the touch** of a sweet and loving man?
How must it feel to have him listen like he's your #1 fan?

Mmmmm, what must love be like when it's true and it's real?
When your eyes roll back in your head and your whisper becomes a squeal.

I can hardly remember the sensation that made you curl your toes.
Your head may not remember but your heart, well it always knows!

I quickly gain my composure, stand tall, and dry my tears
Why there's a whole host of saints encouraging me with their cheers!

I am not the first and I certainly won't be the last.
While my recovery may be sure, it's definitely not fast!

So I fix my gaze on Him for I really need to be strong.
Besides, its only **the touch** of a loving God can keep me from doing wrong!

"Reproduction!"

Definitely, not a fancy title!

In fact, one might say, this is unattractive!

However, this is how we continue to exist, through the process of reproduction.

We journal, we pray, we meditate. We allow God to work on, work in, and work through us. We always come away better than we began. Remember, I said, better, not perfect! And the beauty of the whole process is when we go and share with another.

Look around you…there are soooo many others that need to be encouraged! Reproduce! Refuse to give up! Too many others are depending on you and your experiences. I believe that all of us have at least one book inside of us!

Besides, we don't know how much we know until we teach another! Ask any parent!

"Reproduction!"

Even as a butterfly struggles for its release;
So must I in my quest for my peace!

It's the struggle that puts the color in a butterfly wing;
And it's the pain that makes the heart take courage and sing.

Just like the butterfly when leaving the cocoon,
I have no desire to return to the womb!

Why I'm excited and hopeful with great possibilities.
No, I'm not finished dotting all my 'i's' or crossing all my 't's.

It's just the joy that He's put there and placed in my heart.
It feels good to be following Him and not putting the horse before the cart!

The butterfly emerges with wings that are wet.
He's careful in his discharge; he's just getting set:

Set to take off, to explore, to dream, and to fly;
Why wouldn't anyone want to be like this? I wonder why?

His wings are spreaded wide as he flies towards the sun.
I know how he must be feeling - he flies purposely, on and on!

The sun dries his wings and it serves to make him strong
But *The Son* dries not only my 'wings', He carries me along!

Unlike the butterfly, I have no need to do it myself.
I depend upon my God and His immense wealth.

So we both are now free and as beautiful as can be;
And me, I'm looking to share with others....wait! I see a cocoon in that tree!

And so begins a new cycle!

"He Couldn't Carry His!"

If Jesus needed a friend to help Him carry His cross…how about us? What an awesome display of humanity! The risen savior falling to the ground under the weight of the cross….When I didn't have a support group…..I created one…I needed each and everyone of you!

I dedicate these thoughts, to the many women whose names I do not know. Women who hugged me in the courthouse, the schoolhouse, their house, and my house. To the woman in the car before me who paid for our meal at Burger King! To the woman who bought me gas when I looked silly after pumping more gas than I had money. To the woman who carried my son to gymnastics practice, thank you. To the women who smile and have no idea how penetrating the warmth of your smile is! Thank you! This poem, I give to all these women and these friends in particular, Yvette, Coni, Rhonda, Jodi, Sasc, **_(Natasha, Ruelita)_**, Andy, Thresa, Becky, Editha, Tangy, Valerie, Marilyn, LaTanya, Diane, Margaret, Roseline, Paula, Connie, Pat, Peggy, Cherise, Ed, Mara, Lisa, Betty, Sandy, Rosa, Joyce, Rosie, Sherry, Sheila, Dot, Sharon, Nicole, Ann, Tara, Gwen, Susie, JB, Sandra, Ann, Susan, Ed, Vickie, Camilla, Victoria, Janet, Tina, Teresa, Virginia, Wilhelmina, Carol, Hannah, Nicole, Theresa, Leslie, Michele, Terri, Lois, Ida, Maple, Kathy, Linda, Lydia, Lynda, Pam, Sheryl, Barbara, Melanie, Towonda, Naomi, and Shannon, and more….thanks for helping me carry my cross! Some more than others but we all need each other!

"What A Friend We Have In Jesus!"
Hymn #340

"He Couldn't Carry His!"

I wandered into a church service:

The speaker said, *"take up your cross!"* invoking thoughts of my worst fears.
I can't carry this thing I said….why **Jesus couldn't even carry His**.

I came away feeling hopeless drenched with the speaker's saliva.
The bewildered 'saint' just stared at me like I was a hopeless bother.

She just laid hands on me reciting the onetime, cure-all**, alleluia,thankyoujesus,you'rehealed,takeupyourbedandwalk** prayer!
I straightened my clothes, collected my thoughts, and silently looked for a way to get up out of there!

She followed me saying, "I'm not traditional…I'm very radical, you see."
I thought to myself, radicals accused Jesus and tradition put Him on the tree.

"I believe", she continued, "in the power of His Word,
I just don't have time to explain the significance of His blood.

You're gonna have to believe and do it for yourself.
I have faith for me and mine but for you there's none left."

She continued, "I'm busy doing ministry, yes I'm on the battlefield.
And I know I'm going to heaven, my God is *really* real!

So excuse me while I leave and go and strut my stuff.
I'm just trying to show you that following Him is just not enough.

Why you must believe, have faith, do works, and let your light so shine.
In other words it wouldn't hurt if your life was more like mine!"

I rushed from there feeling sad, amazed at that lady's gall.
I searched for a CD and settled on a message from my friend, Charles Swindoll.

The message was clear and simple, short and to the point.
Jesus like us did suffer and occasionally was out of joint.

When the weight of the cross burdened him, knocking him to the ground.
From out of the shadows, Simon picked it up and never made a sound.

So when my cross gets heavy and I just can't bear the weight.
Jesus simply says to me, "give it to me my child……the weight is too great!"

My fears began to dissipate when I remember Jesus again.
For on the way to Calvary, His Father sent Him a friend.

So, I take up my cross and follow Jesus, having grown over the years.
I trust God to carry me remembering ……..Jesus **couldn't even carry His**!

"DANCING!"

The last thing you want to do when feeling bad is dance. However, one of the first things you want to do when you celebrate is to dance!

I am not known for being a great dancer…but when I dance, I am known for being a *'free'* dancer. I *love* to dance. It's so therapeutic and exciting! I enjoy watching people who not only love to dance but who are free in their movements. Being a good dancer does not necessarily get my attention, I like *'free'* dancers. A free dancer is one who listens to the rhythm of the music and allows the music to speak to his/her body and moves in concert with the music. This will allow you to dance for the pure enjoyment of dancing and not necessarily with a partner. The music is your partner. This will also prevent me from stepping on someone else's toes.

Today, I feel good and *I am* going to dance like no one else is watching!

He is alive and so am I!

If I know anything, I know He has kept me and continues to do so. So I will dance and praise Him for it! *He is worthy of my dance!*

Alleluia!

Let's Dance!

"DANCING!"

There comes a time when you need to rise from beneath your circumstances.
Just dust off your old attitude and learn some new **dances!**

When you **dance** you're free from the remnants of your sin
You're no longer indebted and you can now live again!

No more looking to a man for fun-filled romance,
Just speak to your Spirit and get on up and **dance!**

Don't *Waltz* around your past doing a *Jitterbug* or two.
It's the *"Funky Chicken"* God wants you to do!

No more playing it cool with a *"70's Two-Step"*.
My God was calling for ACTION! Girrrrllll, get some pep!

Now your issues may refuse to leave and be gone.
That's your first indication that you need a new song.

Leaving your past sometimes requires a walk…maybe a run.
But when you get ready to **dance** you know you're ready to have some fun!

Just throw back your head ~ ~ ~ let the rhythm make you glide.
Who cares if you miss a step while doing *"The Electric Slide"*?!

It doesn't matter if you're *"Twisting"* or you look like a *"Robot"* marching.
At some point in your life, you should **dance** like no one else is watching!

Now, you can't **dance** my **dance** 'cause you haven't walked in my shoes.
See…your taste may be *Jazz,* but mine…. it's the *Blues!*

So rejoice in the Lord, throw your hands in the air.
If others don't like it, don't worry, <u>'cause you really don't care!</u>

94

Just **dance** with all your might like old King David did.
And **dance** like your grandma when she took off her scratchy wig!

Who cares what people think, whether it's a foe or a friend.
They don't know why you're **dancing**…..'cause <u>they don't know where you've been!</u>

"His Just Reward!"

When my Dad passed, honestly, I felt like a little girl. I was in the midst of a separation, not knowing it was really a divorce, I was scared of the future, uncertain of the present, and very spooked by the past! I was a wreck! But as I sat in the room waiting for the morticians to arrive and take the remains, I ingested our last couple of conversations. I felt like it was all making sense. Of course I wrote them down as I've always kept notes but one day after almost three years later, I wrote my first piece about my Dad. And what a befitting piece as I think it pretty much captures the essence of who he was as well as our relationship!

My Dad, Willie Frank Bailey

"His Just Reward!"
From the Apple that didn't fall too far from the Tree!

"Daaaadddd, I need…."
"See me early in the morning before I leave."

"But Daaaaaadddd….!!!"
"Be fully dressed", he hasten to add.

Either he was crazy,
And/or I was very lazy.

Regardless, my feet hit the floor out of great respect.
I actually enjoyed the meeting even if it the motivation was a check.

He loved to use money as motivating tool.
And I was a very good student in my Daddy's school!

My Daddy was a hard working man,
Self-taught, self-motivated with a trowel in his hand.

He wasn't particularly distracted by racial segregation
His favorite subject was, "do we need more education?"

My father was known for having a good time.
And in all of Gwinnett County, you couldn't have found a stronger mind.

Needless to say, my father was my mentor,
My provider, my caretaker, and my greatest professor.

I walked like my Daddy, I talked like my Daddy, I mimicked his style.
And there was absolutely no mistaking - I was his favorite child.

I spent my entire life trying to be affirmed unfortunately,
And finally, on his death bed, he gave it to me.

Morphine made him delirious, was he talking out of his head?
I had to lean closer just to hear what he said.

"Your sisters don't understand you, you're as smart as me.
'Cause Resa, you're the apple that did not fall too far from the tree!"

Well Daddy passed on and left me still a little girl.
But reflecting on the affirmation, I was ready to meet the World.

It's time to grow up and leave your past behind.
Forgive, forget! Get out of jail or forever serve the time!

I love you Daddy and I am grateful God gave us each other.
And what a blessing you chose Ms. Evelyn as my Mother.

So what you guys made mistakes from beginning to end.
But my bible tells me that Love covers a multitude of sin.

Well Daddy's gone but I still remember him saying with his cute little grin,
"Hey! Swim on out there! Don't wait for your ship to come in!"

My Daddy loved God's Word and taught me to do the same.
He once paid me $500 to read it, I thought it was a game!

But after he was gone, this same Word strengthened my heart.
And just like he rewarded me, his heavenly Father rewarded him for his part!

You see, now I know He was using my Dad and I say, "thank you Father God!"
And what a comfort it is to know my Daddy got **his just reward!**

Dedicated in remembrance of Willie Frank Bailey
January 27, 1932 ~ February 12, 2001

"TO MY FRIEND AND MY SISTER"

My blood and your blood - no it's definitely not the same.
Butcher, Bailey, McClendon….neither is our name.

You're from the Midwest and I'm from the South.
We speak love for each other with our own mouth.

Our lives run parallel and yet differently.
You're happy being you and I'm happy being me!

It's not what we have in common that binds us so close.
It's the fact that we became sisters and that's what matters most!

We are different in our style and even in our taste.
But each of us would welcome the other in her own space.

I thank my God for giving me a friend for all time.
Jesus Himself modeled this for all of mankind.

So now you're my sister and yes, you're my friend.
I will be there for you and you for me, right to the bitter end.

So what we arrived differently, not from the same womb.
But there's a place for you in my heart, I'll always have room!

It's the blood of Jesus that binds us and keeps us hanging tight.
I'm telling all who listens, they better treat you right!

So no matter who we are and or where we come from;
The World had better get ready 'cause we're taking it by storm!

"................"

Sometimes, when it hurts badly, there are no words to describe our feelings.

"And it was now about the sixth hour, and a darkness came over the whole land until the ninth hour the sun's light failing: and the veil of the temple was rent <u>in the midst</u>."
Luke 23:44-45

    At the death of His only begotten Son, God the Father turned out the lights on the earth, turned His back to the people on the earth, and trashed His church! I mean, He tore it up! I know…..I took some liberties with the Word….but I want us to seriously face the fact that God did grieve for His Son upon His death….*knowing*, He was going to raise Him from the dead!

    If God can grieve over the death of His Son and cause mass destruction, then

    how much do we? It is never easy to attend a funeral and I can not even imagine attending the funeral of your child….especially if it's your only one! I shared with my cousins, Carl and Sheryl at the passing of their young baby, sad and tragic. The conception had produced triplets, Gabriella was the second baby to pass. How hard!!! Today, praise God, only Naiya remains. I dedicate these thoughts to them and so many others.

    But God makes it clear to us that He grieved and it is okay for us to do likewise. *Except*….I think we should add to our knowledge of grief that He really does know, He really does care, and He really does see! With this in mind, we will be all right!

    He knows how we feel when we hurt….He is well aware of what's going on in our lives. It comforts me tremendously when I talk to someone who has a point of reference about my situation. When I speak to someone with no point of reference, I usually walk away condemned. But my bible tells me, 'that there is no condemnation to those that are in Christ Jesus.' *Romans 12:1 KJV*

I was sharing just such a moment with my friend, Susan Dover, when she began to speak. Something in my heart told me to *really* listen and I did. This poem was inspired after listening to her talk about the tough and unexpected circumstances that life presents. I dedicate these thoughts to her as well.

> *"Behold, he that keepeth Israel shall neither slumber nor sleep."*
> *Psalms 121:4*

With her permission, I share:

"................"

Just seeing the tear in your eye
really made me want to cry.

Your voice turned to a whisper when you spoke of your dream
What a small request or so it seemed.

You just want to enjoy your latter days without pain or strife;
while reaping the benefits of a well-planned life.

However, life has challenges and surprises unknown.
Many do not show up until we are grown!

I hasten to add, I empathize, no! I have sympathy for you;
because I can relate when your heart breaks in two.

It is not over, you will agree, for there is this thing called Grace.
That is the stuff that powers us to run in this race.

So I sit back with relief and let out a great big sigh....
That I was not the only one who saw the tear in your eye.

"I Am A Man!"

As a woman, I see things from a woman's perspective more often than not. However, God called us to do the hard things in a relationship or the things that aren't natural. For instance, in the book of Ephesians, the fifth chapter, He tells a woman to respect her husband and the husband to love his wife.

Us women, are not into respect in general. We love to love and we will love anything. We love those shoes, we love your earrings, your jacket, that cute puppy, your bad children, our bad children, and yes, we love our men. But respect, the only men we consciously respect are our bosses, if they are men. We love our pastors! But those bosses, we show up at work on time (for the most part), we do excellent work. We work over time even if we complain behind his back, we do work it. And we dress accordingly. Finally, we do what he asks us to do without grumbling to him.

But our men! That is another story. But we want them to know we love them. God simply says, I know for you love comes easy, that is why I commanded you to respect him, because, "you need me to carry it out!"

Our men, respect each other, the work of other men. They respect other people's stuff lying around, they would never move it! They respect how much other men make, they would never ask. They respect what other men are wearing, they would never make a comment about it even in private with their women. But love! That's a different thing. The only people men love are their mothers! And their women know this! And God says, "you need me to carry it out!"

I was sharing these thoughts with a male friend of mine who did not think He necessarily needed God to do anything but God has a way of capturing your heart and holding it hostage until he, we, me surrenders!

And aren't you glad, He's not gender persuaded?!

Thus, *"I Am A Man!"*

"I Am A Man!"

"You'll be all right. I'm sorry." Seems like vain, empty words.
Especially since I cannot count the times I had already heard,

"You'll be up on your feet, you'll be better in no time…."
It makes one wonder, 'are they trying to comfort or don't want to hear me whine?'

"How dare you speak to me like that don't you know I'm a man?
There's nothing that gets next to me, I can stop it with my hand.

Men like me are tough, we have no need to share…
All this stuff is for women….I'm as strong as a bear!"

I was thinking on all these thoughts trying to grasp the reason for my suffering
And how life could just be fun minus all the heartache it brings.

But that would be such a shallow way to live, like those vain empty words.
It would be like commanding children to action without using verbs!

The suffering builds our muscles and makes us very strong.
We wanted it to happen yesterday. It's just taking a bit too long.

Like most men I flexed my muscles saying, "Who me? Oh I'm all right!
I am a man built strong - I can bench press steel and make it look very light!"

I was doing fine until she came along reciting this particular poem.
Why did she stop right here. Lord get rid of her, make her leave me alone.

But after awhile I felt a rumble, a stirring in my soul
I tried in vain to run from there. I tried to cover my hole.

The hole was in my heart you see. It was getting bigger, I sprung a new

leak.
I can still hear Him saying, "son, you can't run from me, your strength is too weak!."

"Weak! Weak! Who are you calling weak, I can take on any man, it's not hard!"
"That may be true, I'm sure it is, but your arms are too short to box with my God."

I dropped to my knees, and saw water dripping with what I thought was sweat
The wet was different, I touched my face, I just had to check.

I was truly shocked I didn't recognize
The water on my face was tears from my eyes!

As I gain my composure, I thought of my friends and especially my next of kin
I've got to tell them Theresa's book isn't just for women, it's also good for us men!

Theresa was right when she said, 'you'll be alright, now let's go to life's class.'
Then and there I submitted to Him 'cause I knew,
"He really would fit me for the task!"

"He'll Fit You For the Task!"

After reading the stories and poetry, one might ask, "is it possible to have a long lasting, and loving relationship?" It looks extraordinarily hard!

Especially when both people in a relationship are not like me and flawed!

But God guarantees that all is well that ends well. He never promised tranquility on earth, however, He did promise He would never leave not would he ever forsake us. In fact, he informs us we would also have great trials!

"He'll Fit You For the Task" was written to celebrate the marriage of a couple I knew. They were both on their second go around. As I sat listening to the circumstances of their coming together…I realized with deep intensity that the only way they would make it, you can make it, or I can make it is…..God comes along side and equips all us to make it! So what happened to me? Why didn't I feel successful in love?

I pondered these thoughts and it occurred to me that I felt like a failure…but keep in mind, it takes two to tango! The harsh cold stare of the judge is still clear in my mind as he informed me that I was being divorced like it or not! *If God brought me to it, certainly he would bring me through it!* Definitely, I am a witness that He will fit me and you for the task…whether it's marriage, parenting, performing, writing, reading, playing, irregardless. Relationships are God's idea and I, we make a mess of ours but we are reminded everyday, **"He'll Fit Us For the Task!"**

Once again, all I can say is, 'thank you Lord!'

"He'll Fit You For the Task!"

When a man finds a wife, he finds favor with the Lord
That is when that man's maker is the Almighty God.
In fact, more specifically, God says, ***"you found a good thing!"***
Son, you found something more valuable than a gorgeous diamond ring.

'But how can I continually please her the man may well ask".
"That is where I get my Glory", God says, ***"I'll fit you for the ask."***
"You see, a woman is moody, emotional, and likes to have her way.
But a godly woman will submit to a godly man every day!"

"Hello Lord is this conversation just between this man and You?
Or are You ignoring me because I am a woman and beautiful too?"
"Oh no my dear, hold on, I need to put you in check…
Because as usual, you women must learn to treat him with respect."

"But how can I continually serve him the woman may well ask".
"That is where I get my Glory, God says, ***"I'll fit you for the task".***
"My son and my daughter, this union is not the result of man's puny little brain.
Your meeting was all by my arrangement no credit can either of you claim!

You both already know my Son and the joy He brings from me.
Remember through Him and Him alone you will have life eternally.
When things go wrong as they surely will, just lay your problems at His feet.
Because He's the only One who can fix them and make you both complete.

My gift to you at the wedding is a promise that'll make you cry.
You see, I will never leave you, I'm always standing by
The gift will manifest itself greatly when you bow and pray as one.
Because even as it's in your mouth, your request is already done.

So enjoy each other please relax; And know before you ask,
It's not one, it's not the other,
I'm fitting you <u>both</u> for the task!"

"A Tribute to My Auntie"
Ms. Priscilla Bailey Armstrong

My Aunt Priscilla is my Dad's youngest sister. I see her as a strong woman. She could be the inspiration for any number of my poems. She is an absolutely fantastic cook and 'Sweet Blessings' her business is a testimony to that!

I am grateful for my Auntie during my extremely hard time of testing. Of course she opened her home for a refuge and she supported me in every way. God really knows what you need. Because some people haven't been through hard times, it's hard for them to relate when your heart breaks in two but my Auntie has been through some things and she is still standing! She was a single mother for a long time and had to do it without any assistance from a man! She's just one of the many that I know have been successful.

I admire her courage to raise and educate three wonderful daughters and she is now the grandmother of three. She looks terrific! An associate of mine saw me talking to her and assumed she was his age. He was just 15 years off!

I love this woman, she is an inspiration to me. I thank God for preserving this relationship. I am grateful I could offer these few words of tribute to her while she can still hear them. Auntie, I with great respect and love pay tribute to you!

A Tribute to My Auntie

"Who is that fine fox? She's a bad Mamma Jamma!
I turned to look and said, "you nut! That's my Auntie and we call her Hamma!"

But inside I beamed with pride as I watched my Aunt.
The baker of bakers producing all kinds of cakes from layered to bunt!

My father, now deceased, prophesied, "you gonna' be alright."
Little did he know she has the Lord, His Spirit and Might!

Yeah, she's the baby of Jesse and Gladys' clan.
However, her emotional strength has surpassed any Bailey man!

She raised those three girls who turned out well with families of their own.
Now that her nest is empty, with joy she is reaping what she has sown.

When you meet you think she's younger than she looks.
But you know she's much older when you taste the way she cooks.

She is strong, beautiful, and as far as I can tell
She will make her home in Heaven and not up in Hell.

I, myself, am proud that we share the same blood.
Besides, it was her strength that I leaned on when I wallowed in mud!

Her banner to me became, "Resa, you will look back in a year and say, he? Him? Who?"
And to day I can truly say, "Auntie you were right and I am glad that's finally true."

It was good knowing God put her there and she would always say, "child, I understand."

She really massaged me back to health when I was in the sinking sand.

Sometimes she'd call, "Resa, how are you doing? Hold your head high!
If you need to chile, go ahead, I'll listen while you cry!"

So, Auntie, as you move ahead in your life to face another chapter,
I pray God's richest blesses and He grants you what you are after.

May the road ahead be free of junk and unnecessary debris,
And may your ears always be filled with the laughter of your precious grandbabies!

May you always remember from me the thing I am the proudest of,
Is the fact that you are my auntie and please know, from me, you're loved.

"From The Heart Of A Mother"

    This is my send off to my oldest son. Perry has a great call of God on his life and I've really watched in great anticipation! This poem was so easy to write. I wrote it to memorialize his high school graduation. I do look to Perry to walk in his passion and bring the kingdom of God much glory!

    This child has such a terrific sense of humor, I seriously wonder where he got it from. He has been through so much and he is so resilient. I really admire that about him. I love the way he commands and gives respect to his brother. I couldn't ask for a better older son!

    They say the first born gets the best of everything. I'm sure Taylor would agree to that. It's Perry who would take issue, go figure. At any rate, I would appreciate it if you kept Perry in your prayers as the World patiently awaits for his next move, or so he thinks!

"From the Heart of A Mother"

My sweet, my precious, a mother's delight!
The one that I nurtured and the one who will soon take flight!

What a joy you have been to parent, to groom, to polish, and to shine.
To watch you mature and begin to ask rather than whine!

You have caused me great joy and a very little pain,
Nevertheless, ask me over and over, yes! I would do it again.

My heart is full of emotions: sad, happy, and great anticipation,
And yes! I am waiting… waiting like others for the manifestation.

You are an incorporation, you are an empire, and you are a priest!
However, don't forget like Saint Paul, "of sinners you are chief!"

Just remain like any good branch; draw your strength from the stem.
Moreover, most importantly remember the root of it is Him!

It is Christ who gave you your life, your thoughts, and your ideas.
And it is Christ who will handle every single one of your fears.

So, take what you've been taught, what you've seen, and what you've heard;
Never let it be confused with jargon as opposed to the Word!

So move on my son, move swiftly and soar like an eagle in flight,
Always, always remember it is better to do that which is right.

"A Love Story!"

In the exchanged life, He wants us to give Him ours so that He can give us a new one! Let it go! When we hold on to what's no longer ours, what we no longer have any control over, what does not want us, what we do not want, we miss out on what we could really have, let it go! Please!

More often than not, we are missing out on the wonderful things He has planned for us. When Joseph forgave his brothers, they were nowhere around. When the time came for them to come to him, he did not have to struggle, he had released them!

The greatest love stories are the ones when someone gets something they don't deserve. That's what makes us mushy and yearn for more. Usually, we are on the receiving end. I'm looking to be on the giving end. I really want a starring role in a true to life Love Story!

How about you?

Thank you….it's been fun!

Go Well,
Theresa

"A Love Story!"

They were both in their forties on their second go 'round.
They looked forward to getting married in their own hometown.

This time as Christians - they had dated for two years.
It was a new way of living - they had to work through their fears.

Premarital counseling exposed old, new, used, and some borrowed baggage too!
But deliberately and faithfully, they opened each one until they were through.

Stuff was revealed and they cleaned out all of it.
Welllll, if not all, it was really quite a bit!

You see she still wore the band - she bought it for herself.
"It's special!" she declared "I love it and really it's all I have left!"

But it bothered him because she wore it 'with him'.
And 'he' was no longer in the picture, not even in the film.

No date had been set but they knew it would be soon.
When he would pop the question and they would become bride and groom.

At dinner the waitress admired her unique 'wedding band'.
He didn't smile - he looked away. It wasn't for him, it was for 'the other man.'

She was caught up as she professed her undying love. "I'll never take it off!"
He looked startled, he choked, he began to cough!

He collected himself as he drank from his glass.
She sighed with relief waiting for this moment to pass.

"Do you love your ring" he asked, "more than you do me?"
"Honey" she replied, "the only thing I love better is when you and I become we."

"Then please give me your ring and put it in my hand.
I want no more evidence of that other man."

"Baby! Don't do this! You know I love you!
Ask me for anything. Whatever else you ask, I promise I'll do!"

"I see" he sighed as he motioned for the bill.
It seemed like an eternity as both their hearts stood still.

They drove on in silence as they came closer to her house.
Her voice was very quiet like a timid little mouse.

"Honey, I am so sorry, it's such a simple thing.
No request is too great - please, just take the ring."

His eyes were moist for he knew he was really loved.
Nothing or no one was loved greater except their Lord above.

He turned to face her now, with huge tears in his eyes.
He gave her a small package saying, "I have for you a surprise!"

She gasped! She screamed! She cried out in delight!
It looked like her old ring - No! That couldn't be right!

But on closer inspection, it was easier to see;
The new ring laced with diamonds read,
'Now I know, you only love me!'

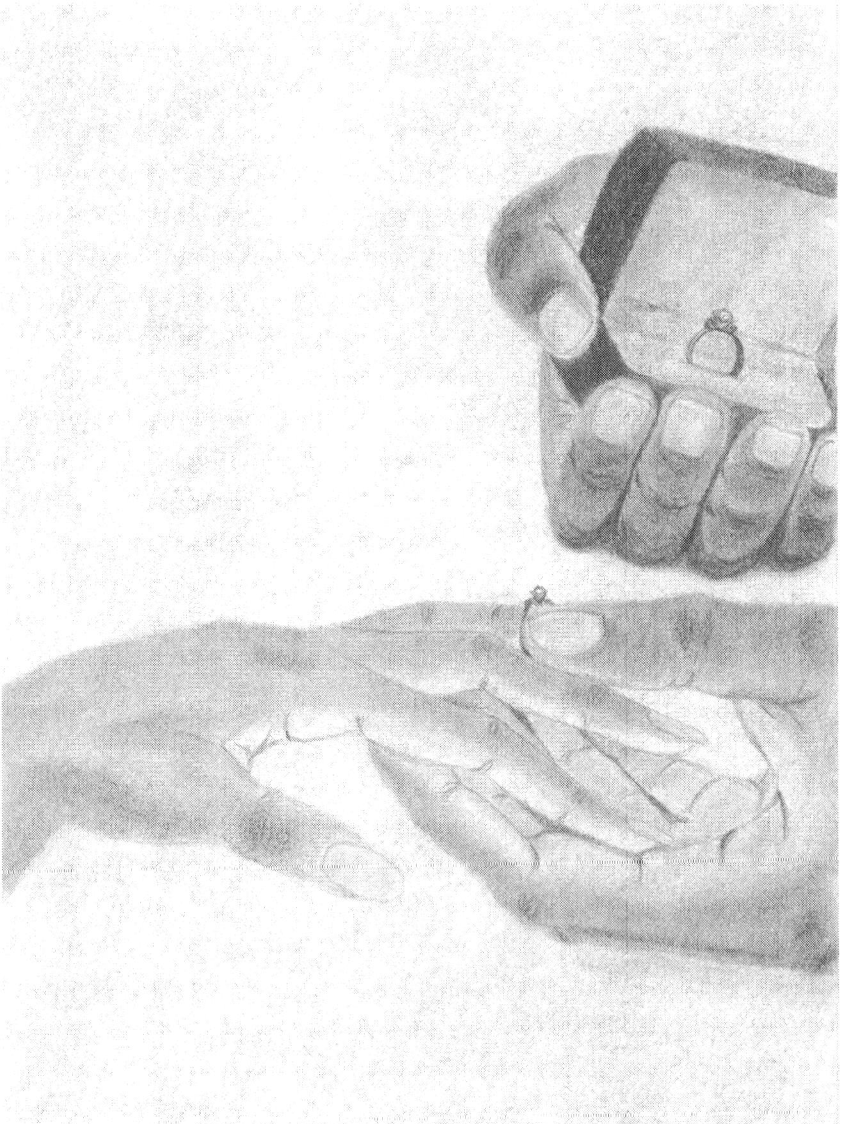

*"**Now**.....it <u>all</u> makes sense!"*

*"The suffering
you sent me
was good
for me,
for
it
taught
me
to pay attention
to your principles."*
Psalms 119:71 NLT

Or as King James would say, *"...it is good that I was afflicted..."*

From My Counselor

I asked my counselor Marilyn Hardin to write a few words regarding counseling.

What gratitude I have to God that I know and have had the opportunity to talk and pray with Theresa McClendon. What pleasure it is to see the awesome creativity of God in making someone as soul rich as Theresa.

I started prayer-counseling in 1980 in the Los Angeles area. What a wonderful adventure it has been. I graduated from Carson-Newman College in 1976. I was overwhelmingly intrigued with how God transforms the human soul. Psychology, interestingly enough, is the very best that man can do. But what I long for is what God desires and lends His power to transform.

I have taken many courses from a diversity of Christian sources all of which have been interesting. My favorite sources have been John and Paula Sandford and their son, Mark Sandford. Leanne Payne, Rita Bennett and Dr. Ed Smith have also been influential to me in my professional walk. But always, I want the bottom line to be, within the context of scripture, *"let's hear from God and receive what He is doing!"*

Marilyn Hardin
Pastoral Counselor

I recommend Marilyn Hardin

Two is Better than One but Three is the Best!

"Two people can accomplish more than twice as much as one; they get a better return for their labor. If one person falls, the other can reach out and help. But people who are alone when they fall are in real trouble. And on a cold night, two under the same blanket can gain warmth from each other. But how can one be warm along? A person standing alone can be attacked and defeated, but two can stand back-to-back and conquer. Three are even better, for a triple-braided cord is not easily broken."

Ecclesiastes 4:9-12 NLT

Betray the Silence. It's absolutely critical that you talk to someone. Expose the perpetrator. It does not matter how many times violence has occurred, one is enough! Call the National Domestic Violence Hotline at 800-799-SAFE. There are trained individuals waiting to assist you with shelter, transportation, and other vital services. Tell someone immediately.

Get Support. There are trained advocates all over this country most of whom offer free services. Lean on your family, friends, church, or get in a support group. If there is not support group, be ready to start one!

Know the Signs. You know your mate or partner. You know what sets them off. Pay close attention. If he or she will not commit to counseling, this is a sign. You must be the one to make the move. Don't play with fiery tempers. Know within your mind your plan of escape. Have an emergency plan. Always have someone with whom you can speak very frankly to. Keep a cell phone close to you. **(You may access 911 from a deactivated cell phone).** Have an emergency bag with clothes and other necessities at a trusted friend's house for you and your kids. Keep at least a half of tank of gas in your car. Keep some extra cash just for this purpose. Memorize key phone numbers. Be alert! *"Devote yourself to prayer with an alert mind and a thankful heart."* Col. 4:1 NLT

If your friend is the victim. Be a friend. Reference *Ecclesiastes 4:9-12*. Do not chide, chastise or accuse. Offer to him/her your every available resource. Assist with childcare, transportation, doctor's appointments, house cleaning, financial matters, decision making, and pray. <u>Withhold advice.</u> *<u>People don't care how much you know until they know how much you care.</u>* While in the victim mode, it is next to impossible to hear advice. Your primary goal is to establish or build on your relationship for the purposes of trust and accountability. Your friend needs you and you need your friend. It is a growing process for both of you. Be content to show you care.

Counseling

Who needs counseling?
Those who cannot function from day to day, poor decision making or unable to make even simple decisions, experiencing compound losses at the same time, more than one loss, recent death, dramatic weight loss or gain, dramatic drop in standard of living.

Where to find counseling?
Ministers, referrals, Christian radio, television, Christian publications, local agencies, hospitals, support groups, churches, word of mouth, refer to the Resource list at the back of this book, and books like "*In The Midst Of....*"

What to look for in a counselor?
Someone who shares your faith, verified credentials in psychology, balanced approach that includes attention to physical, emotional, intellectual, and spiritual issues; someone who can communicate clearly with you regarding goals, findings, and possible duration of counseling; someone who specializes in a particular interest, chemical dependence, victimization, child play therapy, spiritual counsel, divorce recovery, etc.

How to pay for counseling?
Most insurance plans share in part of the cost, ability to pay, sometimes it's free of charge; some allow to pay as you go along; exchange some service (cleaning, painting, baking, etc); solicit from family and friends, use money that used to be used on habits; borrow money - it's a great investment for your family!

RESOURCES

I recommend anything by Drs Henry Cloud and John Townsend
　　www.drhenrycloud.com

I recommend the ministry of "Insight for Living" with Charles Swindoll
　　www.insight.org

I recommend the ministry of Focus On the Family with Dr. James Dobson
　　www.focusonthefamily.org

I recommend the ministry of Family Life Today with Dennis Rainey
　　www.fltoday.org

I recommend the ministry of New Birth Missionary Baptist with Bishop Eddie Long
　　www.newbirth.org

I recommend the ministry of T. D. Jakes especially "Woman Thou Art Loosed Conf"
　　www.tdjakes.org

I recommend the ministry of Living Proof Ministries with Beth Moore
　　www.bethmoore.org

I recommend the ministry of In Touch with Dr. Charles Stanley
　　www.intouch.org

I recommend the ministry of The Urban Alternative with Dr. Tony Evans
　　www.tonyevans.org

I recommend the ministry of Your local church, small groups, and Sunday Church School. Be faithful at home, first!

My reading list is endless: Begin with God's Word, several versions. My favorites are the New Living Testament and The New American Standard Bible. Any of the following authors offered tremendous insight, wisdom, and instruction for me: Jeff VanVonderen, David Seamands, Max Lucado, David Collins, Liz Curtis Higgs, Joyce Meyer, Robert McGee, Stormie Omartian, John Maxwell, **Theresa Bailey McClendon** and many more!

I recommend absolutely great music: My favorites are Shirley Caesar, Donna McClurkin, Babbie Mason, James Bignon, Steven Curtis Chapman, Jars of Clay, Fred Hammond, Kurt Carr, Aaron Neville, Albertina Walker, Mary Mary, Donald Lawrence, Rance Allen, Shirley Murdock, Yolanda Adams, etc. and your local church choirs or groups!

*"ONCE
A
CATERPILLAR
BECOMES
A
BUTTERFLY,
IT
WILL
NEVER
CRAWL
AGAIN!"*

Not The End but The Beginning!

Made in the USA
Charleston, SC
22 February 2013